The Summer
Without Men

Also by Siri Hustvedt

Siri Hustvedt

The Summer
Without Men

SCEPTRE

First published in Great Britain in 2011 by Sceptre
An imprint of Hodder & Stoughton
An Hachette UK company

First published in the United States in 2011 by Henry Holt

6

A CIP catalogue record for this title is
available from the British Library.

Hardback ISBN 978 1 444 71052 6
Paperback ISBN 978 1 444 71054 0

Typeset in 12.5/15.5pt Monotype Sabon by
Palimpsest Book Production Limited, Falkirk, Stirlingshire

Printed and bound by Clays Ltd, St Ives plc

Hodder & Stoughton policy is to use papers that are natural,
renewable and recyclable products and made from wood grown
in sustainable forests. The logging and manufacturing processes are expected
to conform to the environmental regulations of the country of origin.

Hodder & Stoughton Ltd
338 Euston Road
London NW1 3BH

www.hodder.co.uk

Illustrations by the author © Siri Hustvedt 2011

For Frances Cohen

LUCY (IRENE DUNNE): You're all confused, aren't you?
JERRY (CARY GRANT): Uh-huh. Aren't you?
LUCY: No.
JERRY: Well, you should be, because you're wrong about things being different because they're not the same. Things are different, except in a different way. You're still the same, only I've been a fool. Well, I'm not now. So, as long as I'm different, don't you think things could be the same again? Only a little different.

—*The Awful Truth*
directed by Leo McCarey
screenplay by Viña Delmar

Sometime after he said the word *pause,* I went mad and landed in the hospital. He did not say *I don't ever want to see you again* or *It's over,* but after thirty years of marriage *pause* was enough to turn me into a lunatic whose thoughts burst, ricocheted, and careened into one another like popcorn kernels in a microwave bag. I made this sorry observation as I lay on my bed in the South Unit, so heavy with Haldol I hated to move. The nasty rhythmical voices had grown softer, but they hadn't disappeared, and when I closed my eyes I saw cartoon characters racing across pink hills and disappearing into blue forests. In the end, Dr. P. diagnosed me with Brief Psychotic Disorder, also known as Brief Reactive Psychosis, which means that you are genuinely crazy but not for long. If it goes on for more than one month, you need another label. Apparently, there's often a trigger or, in psychiatric parlance, "a stressor," for this particular form of derangement. In my case, it was Boris or, rather, the fact that there was no Boris, that Boris was having his pause. They kept me locked up for a week and a half, and then they let me go. I was an outpatient for a while before I found Dr. S., with her low musical voice, restrained smile, and good ear for poetry. She propped me up—still props me up, in fact.

I don't like to remember the madwoman. She shamed me. For a long time, I was reluctant to look at what she had written in a black-and-white notebook during her stay on the ward. I knew what was scrawled on the outside in handwriting that looked nothing like mine, *Brain shards,* but I wouldn't open it. I was afraid of her, you see. When my girl came to visit, Daisy hid her unease. I don't know exactly what she saw, but I can guess: a woman gaunt from not eating, still confused, her body wooden from drugs, a person who couldn't respond appropriately to her daughter's words, who couldn't hold her own child. And then, when she left, I heard her moan to the nurse, the noise of a sob in her throat: "It's like it's not my mom." I was lost to myself then, but to recall that sentence now is an agony. I do not forgive myself.

The Pause was French with limp but shiny brown hair. She had significant breasts that were real, not manufactured, narrow rectangular glasses, and an excellent mind. She was young, of course, twenty years younger than I was, and my suspicion is that Boris had lusted after his colleague for some time before he lunged at her significant regions. I have pictured it over and over. Boris, snow-white locks falling onto his forehead as he grips the bosom of said Pause near the cages of genetically modified rats. I always see it in the lab, although this is probably wrong. The two of them were rarely alone there, and the "team" would have noticed noisy grappling in their midst. Perhaps they took refuge in a toilet stall, my Boris pounding away at his fellow scientist, his eyes moving upward in their sockets as he neared explosion. I knew all about it. I had seen his eyes roll thousands of times. The banality of the story—the fact that it is repeated every day ad nauseam by men who discover all at once or gradually that what IS does not HAVE TO BE and then act to free themselves from the aging women who have taken care of them and their children for years—does not mute the misery, jealousy, and humiliation that comes over those left behind. Women scorned. I wailed and shrieked and beat the wall with my fists. I frightened him. He wanted peace, to be left alone to go his own way with the well-mannered neuroscientist of his dreams, a woman with whom he had no past, no freighted pains, no grief, and no conflict. And yet he said *pause,* not *stop,* to keep the narrative open, in case he changed his mind. A cruel crack of hope. Boris, the Wall. Boris, who never shouts. Boris shaking his head on the sofa, looking discomfited. Boris, the rat man who married a poet in 1979. Boris, why did you leave me?

I had to get out of the apartment because being there hurt. The rooms and furniture, the sounds from the street, the light that shone into my study, the tooth-brushes in the small rack, the bedroom closet with its missing knob—each had become like a bone that ached, a joint or rib or vertebrae in an articulated anatomy of shared memory, and each familiar thing, leaden with the accumulated meanings of time, seemed to weigh in my own body, and I found I could not bear them. And so I left Brooklyn and went home for the summer to the backwater town on what used to be the prairie in Minnesota, out where I had grown up. Dr. S. was not against it. We would have telephone sessions once a week except during August, when she took her usual vacation. The University had been "understanding" about my crack-up, and I would return to teaching in September. This was to be the Yawn between Crazed Winter and Sane Fall, an uneventful hollow to fill with poems. I would spend time with my mother and put flowers on my father's grave. My sister and Daisy would come for visits, and I had been hired to teach a poetry class for kids at the local Arts Guild. "Award-Winning Home-Grown Poet Offers Workshop" ran a headline in the *Bonden News*. The Doris P. Zimmer Award for Poetry is an obscure prize that dropped down on my head from nowhere, offered exclusively to a woman whose work falls under the rubric "experimental." I had accepted this dubious honor and the check that accompanied it graciously but with private reservations only to find that ANY prize is better than none, that the term "award-winning" offers a useful, if purely decorative gloss on the poet who lives in a world that knows nothing of poems. As John Ashbery once said, "Being a famous poet is the not the same thing as being famous." And I am not a famous poet.

I rented a small house at the edge of town not far from my mother's apartment in a building exclusively for the old and the very old. My mother lived in the independent zone. Despite arthritis and various other complaints, including occasional bursts of dangerously high blood pressure, she was remarkably spry and clear-headed at eighty-seven. The complex included two other distinct zones—for those who needed help, "assisted living," and the "care center," the end of the line. My father had died there six years earlier and, although I had once felt a tug to return and look at the place again, I had gotten no farther than the entryway before I turned around and fled from the paternal ghost.

"I haven't told anybody here about your stay in the hospital," my mother said in an anxious voice, her intense green eyes holding mine. "No one has to know."

I shall forget the drop of Anguish
that scalds me now—that scalds me now!

Emily Dickinson No. #193 to the rescue. Address: Amherst.

Lines and phrases winged their way into my head all summer long. "If a thought without a thinker comes along," Wilfred Bion said, "it may be what is a 'stray thought' or it could be a thought with the owner's name and address upon it, or it could be a 'wild thought.' The problem, should such a thing come along, is what to do with it."

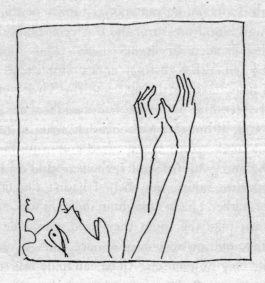

There were houses on either side of my rental—new development domiciles—but the view from the back window was unobstructed. It consisted of a small backyard with a swing set and behind it a cornfield, and beyond that an alfalfa field. In the distance was a copse of trees, the outlines of a barn, a silo, and above them the big, restless sky. I liked the view, but the interior of the house disturbed me, not because it was ugly but because it was dense with the lives of its owners, a pair of young professors with two children who had absconded to Geneva for the summer on some kind of research grant. When I put down my bag and boxes of books and looked around, I wondered how I would fit myself into this place, with its family photographs and decorative pillows of unknown Asian origin, its rows of books on government and world courts and diplomacy, its boxes of toys, and the lingering smell of cats, blessedly not in residence. I had the grim thought that there had seldom been room for me and mine, that I had been a scribbler of the stolen interval. I had worked at the kitchen table in the early days and run to Daisy when she woke from her nap. Teaching and the poetry of my students—poems without urgency, poems dressed up in "literary" curlicues and ribbons—had run away with countless hours. But then, I hadn't fought for myself or, rather, I hadn't fought in the right way. Some people just take the room they need, elbowing out intruders to take possession of a space. Boris could do it without moving a muscle. All he had to do was stand there "quiet as a mouse." I was a noisy mouse, one of those that scratched in the walls and made a ruckus, but somehow it made no difference. The magic of authority, money, penises.

I put every framed picture carefully into a box, noting on a small piece of tape where each one belonged. I folded up several rugs and stored them with about twenty superfluous pillows and children's games, and then I methodically cleaned the house, excavating clumps of dust to which paper clips, burnt matchsticks, grains of cat litter, several smashed M&Ms, and unidentifiable bits of debris had adhered themselves. I bleached the three sinks, the two toilets, the bathtub, and the shower. I scoured the kitchen floor, dusted and washed the ceiling lamps, which were thick with grime. The purge lasted two days and left me with sore limbs and several cuts on my hands, but the savage activity left the rooms sharpened. The musty, indefinite edges of every object in my visual field had taken on a precision and clarity that cheered me, at least momentarily. I unpacked my books, set myself up in what appeared to be the husband's study (clue: pipe paraphernalia), sat down, and wrote:

> Loss.
> A known absence.
> If you did not know it,
> it would be nothing,
> which it is, of course,
> a nothing of another kind,
> as acutely felt as a blister,

but a tumult, too,
in the region of the heart and lungs,
an emptiness with a name: You.

My mother and her friends were widows. Their husbands had mostly been dead for years, but they had lived on and during that living on had not forgotten their departed men, though they didn't appear to clutch at memories of their buried spouses, either. In fact, time had made the old ladies formidable. Privately, I called them the Five Swans, the elite of Rolling Meadows East, women who had earned their status, not through mere durability or a lack of physical problems (they all ailed in one way or the other), but because the Five shared a mental toughness and autonomy that gave them a veneer of enviable freedom. George (Georgiana), the oldest, acknowledged that the Swans had been lucky. "We've all kept our marbles so far," she quipped. "Of course, you never know—we always say that anything can happen at any moment." The woman had lifted her right hand from her walker and snapped her fingers. The friction was feeble, however, and generated no sound, a fact she seemed to recognize because her face wrinkled into an asymmetrical smile.

I did not tell George that my marbles had been lost and found, that losing them had scared me witless, or that as I stood chatting with her in the long hallway a line from another George, Georg Trakl, came to me: *In kühlen Zimmern ohne Sinn*. In cool rooms without sense. In cool senseless rooms.

"Do you know how old I am?" she continued.

"One hundred and two years old."

She owned a century.

"And Mia, how old are you?"

"Fifty-five."

"Just a child."

Just a child.

There was Regina, eighty-eight. She had grown up in Bonden but fled the provinces and married a diplomat. She had lived in several countries, and her diction had an estranged quality—overly enunciated perhaps—the result both of repeated dips in foreign environs and, I suspected, pretension, but that self-conscious additive had aged along with the speaker until it could no longer be separated from her lips or tongue or teeth. Regina exuded an operatic mixture of vulnerability and charm. Since her husband's death, she had been married twice—both men dropped dead—and thereafter followed several entanglements with men, including a dashing Englishman ten years younger than she was. Regina relied on my mother as confidante and fellow sampler of local cultural events—concerts, art shows, and the occasional play. There was Peg, eighty-four, who was born and raised in Lee, a town even smaller than Bonden, met her husband in high school, had six children with him, and had acquired multitudes of grandchildren she managed to keep track of in infinitesimal detail, a sign of striking neuronal health. And finally there was Abigail, ninety-four. Though she'd once been tall, her spine had given way to osteoporosis, and the woman hunched badly. On top of that, she was nearly deaf, but from my first glimpse of her, I had felt admiration. She dressed in neat pants and sweaters of her own handiwork, appliquéd or embroidered with apples or horses or dancing children. Her husband was long gone—dead, some said; others maintained it was divorce. Whichever it was, Private Gardener had vanished during or just after the Second World War, and his widow or divorcée had acquired a teaching degree and become a grade school art teacher. "Crooked and deaf, but not dumb," she had said emphatically upon our first meeting. "Don't hesitate to visit. I like the company. It's three-two-oh-four. Repeat after me, three-two-oh-four."

The five were all readers and met for a book club with a few other women once a month, a gathering that had, I gleaned from various sources, a somewhat competitive edge to it. During the time my mother had lived in Rolling Meadows, any number of characters in the theater of her everyday life had left the stage for "Care," never to return. My mother told me frankly that once a person left the premises, she vanished into "a black hole." Grief was minimal. The Five lived in a ferocious present because unlike the young, who entertain their finality in a remote, philosophical way, these women knew that death was not abstract.

* * *

Had it been possible to keep my ugly disintegration from my mother, I would have done it, but when one family member is hauled off and locked up in the bin, the others surge forth with their concern and pity. What I had wanted terribly to hide from Mama I was able freely to show my sister, Beatrice. She received the news and, two days after my admission to the South Unit, hopped a plane to New York. I didn't see them open the glass doors for her. My attention must have wandered for an instant because I had been waiting and watching for her arrival. I think she spotted me right away because I looked up when I heard the determined clicking of her high heels as she marched toward me, sat down on the oddly slippery sofa in the common area, and put her arms around me. As soon as I felt her fingers squeeze my arms, the choking dryness of the antipsychotic cocoon I had been living in broke to pieces, and I sobbed loudly. Bea rocked me and stroked my head. Mia, she said, my Mia. By the time Daisy returned for a second visit, I was sane. The ruin had been at least partially rebuilt, and I did not wail in front of her.

Crying jags, howling, screeches, and laughter for no reason were not at all uncommon on the Unit and mostly passed unnoticed. Insanity is a state of profound self-absorption. An extreme effort is required just to keep track of one's self, and the turn toward wellness happens the moment a bit of the world is allowed back in, when a person or thing passes through the gate. Bea's face. My sister's face.

My breakdown pained Bea, but I was afraid it would kill my mother. It didn't.

Sitting across from her in the small apartment, I had the thought that my mother was a place for me as well as a person. The Victorian family house on the corner of Moon Street where my parents had lived for over forty years, with its spacious parlor rooms and warren of bedrooms upstairs, had been sold after my father's death, and when I walked past it, the loss pained me as if I were still a child who couldn't make sense of some upstart occupying her old haunts. But it was my mother herself whom I had come home to. There is no living without a ground, without a sense of space that is not only external but internal—mental loci. For me, madness had been suspension. When Boris abruptly took his body and his voice away, I began to float. One day, he blurted out his wish for a *pause*, and that was all. No doubt he had meditated on his decision, but I had had no part in his deliberations. A man goes out for cigarettes and never returns. A man tells his wife he is taking a stroll and doesn't come home for dinner—ever again. One day in winter the man just up and left. Boris had not articulated his unhappiness, had never told me he didn't want me. It just came over him. Who were these men? After I had pieced myself together with "professional help," I returned to older, more reliable territory, to the Land of M.

It was true that Mama's world had shrunk, and she had shrunk with it. She ate too little, I thought. When left to her own devices, she assembled large plates of raw carrots and peppers and cucumbers with perhaps one tiny piece of fish or ham or cheese. For years the woman had cooked and baked enough for armies and stored the foodstuffs in a gigantic freezer in the basement. She had sewn our dresses, mended our wool stockings, shined copper and brass until it gleamed bright and hard. She had curled butter for parties, arranged flowers, hung out and ironed sheets that smelled of clean sun when you slept in them. She had sung to us at night, handed us edifying reading material, censored movies, and defended her daughters to uncomprehending schoolteachers. And when we were sick, she would make a bed for the ailing child on the floor near her while she did the housework. I loved being unwell with Mama, not vomiting or truly miserable perhaps, but in a state of recovery by increments. I loved to lie on the special bed and feel Mama's hand on my forehead, which she then moved up into my sweaty hair as she checked the fever. I loved to sense her legs moving near me, to listen to her voice take on that special intonation for the invalid, songlike and tender, which would make me want to stay ill, to lie there forever on the little pallet, pale, Romantic, and pathetic, half me, half swooning actress, but always securely orbited by my mother.

Sometimes now, her hands shook in the kitchen and a plate or spoon would drop suddenly to the floor.

She remained elegant and immaculate in her dress, but worried terribly over spots, wrinkles, and shoes that were improperly shined, something I didn't remember from when I was young. I think the shining house had gone inward and been replaced by shining garments. Her memory sometimes lapsed, but only about recent incidents or sentences just uttered. The early days of her life had an acuity that seemed almost supernatural. As she aged, I did more and she did less, but this change in our rapport seemed minor. Although the indefatigable champion of domesticity had vanished, the woman who had fixed up a little bed to keep her sick children near her sat across from me, undiminished.

"I always thought you felt too much," she said, repeating a family theme, "that you were overly sensitive, a princess on the pea, and now with Boris . . ." My mother's expression turned rigid. "How could he? He's over sixty. He must be crazy . . ." She glanced at me and put her hand over her mouth.

I laughed.

"You're still beautiful," my mother said.

"Thanks, Mama." The comment was no doubt meant for Boris. How could you desert the *still beautiful*? "I want you to know," I said, in answer to nothing, "that the doctors really say I am recovered, that this can happen and then never happen again. They believe that I have returned to myself—just a garden-variety neurotic—nothing more."

"I think teaching that little class will do you good.

Are you looking forward to it at all?" Her voice cracked with feeling—hope mingled with anxiety.

"Yes," I said. "Although I've never taught children."

My mother was silent, then said, "Do you think Boris will get over it?"

The "it" was actually a "she," but I appreciated my mother's tact. We would not give it a name. "I don't know," I said. "I don't know what goes on in him. I never have."

My mother nodded sadly, as if she knew all about it, as if this turn in my marriage were part of a world script she had glimpsed long ago. Mama, the Sage. The reverberations of felt meaning moved like a current through her thin body. This had not changed.

As I walked down the hallway of Rolling Meadows East, I found myself humming and then singing softly,

> *Twinkle, twinkle, little bat!*
> *How I wonder what you're at!*
> *Up above the world you fly,*
> *Like a tea-tray in the sky.*

I managed the mornings of that first week, working quietly at the borrowed desk, then reading for a couple of hours until the afternoon visits and long talks with my mother. I listened to her stories about Boston and my grandparents, to her recitation of the idyllic routines of her middle-class childhood, disrupted now and again by her brother Harry, an imp, not a revolutionary, who died at twelve of polio when my mother was nine and changed her world. She had told herself on that day in December to write down everything she remembered about Harry, and she did it for months on end. "Harry couldn't keep his feet still. He was always swinging them against the chair legs at breakfast." "Harry had a freckle on his elbow that looked like a tiny mouse." "I remember Harry cried in the closet once so I couldn't see him."

I cooked dinner for Mama most evenings at my place or hers, feeding her well with meat and potatoes and pasta, and then I walked over the moist grass into the rented house where I raged alone. Sturm und Drang. Whose play was that? Friedrich von Klinger. Kling. Klang. Bang. Mia Fredricksen in revolt against the Stressor. Storm and Stress. Tears. Pillow beating. Monster Woman blasts into space and bursts into bits that scatter and settle over the little town of Bonden. The grand theater of Mia Fredricksen in torment with no audience but the walls, not her Wall, not Boris Izcovich, traitor, creep, and beloved. Not He. Not B.I. No sleep but for pharmacology and its dreamless oblivion.

"The nights are hard," I said. "I just keep thinking about the marriage."

I could hear Dr. S. breathe. "What kind of thoughts?"

"Fury, hatred, and love."

"That's succinct," she said.

I imagined her smiling but said, "I hate him. I got an e-mail: 'How are you, Mia? Boris.' I wanted to send back a big gob of my saliva."

"Boris is probably feeling guilty, don't you think, and worried. I would guess that he's confused, too, and from what you told me Daisy has been awfully angry with him, and that must cut pretty deep. It's obvious that he's not a person who does well with conflict. There are reasons for that, Mia. Think of his family, his brother. Think of Stefan's suicide."

I didn't answer her. I remembered Boris's hollow voice on the phone saying he had found Stefan dead. I remembered the yellow note stuck to the kitchen wall that said, "Call plumber" and that each letter of that reminder had an alien quality as if it weren't English. It had made no sense, but the voice in my head had been crisp, matter-of-fact: *You must call the police and go to him now.* No confusion, no panic, but an awareness that the terrible thing had come and that I felt hard. This has happened; it is true. You must act now. There were drops of rain on the cab window, then sudden thin slides of water, behind which I could see the fogged buildings downtown and then the street sign for N. Moore, so ordinary, so familiar. The elevator with its cold gray panels, the low ringing sound at the third floor. Stefan hanging. The word *No.* Then again. *No.* Boris throwing up in the bathroom. My hand stroking his head, gripping his shoulders firmly. He didn't weep; he grunted in my arms like a hurt animal.

"It was terrible," I said in a flat voice.

"Yes."

"I took care of him. I held him up. What would he have done if I hadn't been there? How can he not remember? He turned into a stone. I fed him. I talked to him. I tolerated his silence. He refused to get help. He went to the lab, ran the experiments, came home, and turned back into a rock. Sometimes I worry that I'll incinerate myself with my anger. I'll just blow up. I'll break down again."

"Blowing up is not the same as breaking down and, as we've said before, even breaking down can have its purpose, its meanings. You held yourself together for a long time, but tolerating cracks is part of being well and alive. I think you're doing that. You don't seem so afraid of yourself."

"I love you, Dr. S."

"I'm glad to hear that."

I heard the child before I saw her: a small voice that came from behind a bush. "I'm putting you in the garden, that's it, and you mustn't be sillies or willies or dillies . . . Absolutely not! Plop, here, here. Yes, look, a hill for you. Dandelion trees. Teeny wind blowing. Okay, peoples, a house."

From my reclining position in the lawn chair where I was reading, I saw a pair of short, naked legs come into view, take two steps, and then drop to a kneeling position on the ground. The partly visible child had a green plastic bucket, which she dumped out on the grass. I saw a pink dollhouse and a host of figures, hard and stuffed, of various sizes, and then the girl's head, which startled me before I understood that she was wearing a fright wig of some kind, a gnarled platinum concoction that made me think of an electrocuted Harpo Marx. The commentary resumed. "You can get in, Ratty, and you too, Beary. Look, you talk to each others. Some dishes." Running exit, swift return, spillage of small cups and plates onto the grass. Busy arrangements and then chewing noises, lip smacking, and simulated burps. "It's not polite to burp at the table. See, he's coming, it's Giraffey. Can you fit in? Squeeze in there." Giraffey did not fit well, so his manipulator settled for the entrance of the fellow's head and neck in-house, body beyond.

I returned to my book, but the child's voice pulled me away now and again by small exclamations and loud humming. A brief silence was followed by a sudden lament: "Too bad I'm real so I can't go in my little house and live!"

I remembered, remembered that threshold world of Almost, where wishes are nearly real. Could it be that my dolls stirred at night? Had the spoon moved of its own accord a fraction of an inch? Had my hope enchanted it? The real and unreal like mirror twins, so close to each other they both breathed living breaths. Some fear, too. You had to brush against the uneasy sense that dreams had broken out of their confinement in sleep and pushed into daylight. Don't you wish, Bea said, the ceiling was the floor? Don't you wish we could . . .

The girl was standing about five feet away, staring gravely in my direction, a round and sturdy person of three or four with a moon face and big eyes under the ludicrous wig. In one hand, she gripped Giraffey by the neck, a battle-scarred creature who looked as if he needed hospitalization.

"Hi," I said. "What's your name?"

She shook her head vigorously, puffed out her cheeks, turned suddenly, and ran.

Too bad I'm real, I thought.

My bout of nerves before meeting my poetry class of seven pubescent girls struck me as ridiculous, and yet I could feel the constriction in my lungs, hear my shallow breaths, the small puffs of my anxiety. I spoke sternly to myself. You have taught graduate school students writing for years, and these are only children. Also, you should have known that no self-respecting boy of Bonden would sign up for a poetry workshop, that out here in the provinces, poetry signifies frails, dolls, and dowagers. Why would you expect to attract more than a few girls with vague and probably senti-mental fantasies about writing verse? Who was I anyway? I had my Doris prize and I had my PhD in comparative literature and my job at Columbia, crusts of respectability to offer as evidence that my failure wasn't complete. The trouble with me was that the inside had touched the outside. After crumbling to bits, I had lost that brisk confidence in the wheels of my own mind, the realization that had come to me sometime in my late forties that I might be ignored, but I could out-think just about anybody, that massive reading had turned my brain into a synthetic machine that could summon philosophy and science and literature in the same breath. I roused myself with a list of mad poets (some more and some less): Torquato Tasso, John Clare, Christopher Smart, Friedrich Hölderlin, Antonin Artaud, Paul Celan, Randall Jarrell, Edna St. Vincent Millay, Ezra Pound, Robert Fergusson, Velimir Khlebnikov, Georg Trakl, Gustaf Fröding, Hugh MacDiarmid, Gérard de Nerval, Edgar Allan Poe, Burns Singer, Anne Sexton, Robert Lowell, Theodore Roethke, Laura Riding, Sara Teasdale, Vachel Lindsay, John Berryman, James Schuyler, Sylvia Plath, Delmore Schwartz . . . Buoyed by the reputations of my fellow maniacs, depressives, and voice hearers, I hopped on my bicycle to meet the seven poetic flowers of Bonden.

As I looked around the table at my pupils, I grew calmer. They were indeed children. The preposterous but poignant realities of girls on the cusp asserted themselves immediately, and my sympathy for them almost choked me. Peyton Berg, several inches taller than I, very thin, with no breasts, constantly adjusted her arms and legs as if they were alien limbs. Jessica

Lorquat was tiny, but she had the body of a woman. A false atmosphere of femininity hung about her that made itself known chiefly in an affectation—a cooing baby voice. Ashley Larsen, sleek brown hair, slightly protruding eyes, walked and sat with the self-conscious air that comes with a newly acquired erogenous zone—holding herself chest-out to display growing buds. Emma Hartley withdrew behind a veil of blond hair, smiling shyly. Nikki Borud and Joan Kavacek, both plump and loud, appeared to function in tandem, as one giggling, mincing persona. Alice Wright, pretty, large teeth covered by braces, was reading when I came in and continued to read quietly until the class started. When she closed the book, I saw that it was *Jane Eyre,* and I felt a moment of envy, the envy of first discovery.

At least one of them was wearing perfume, which on the warm June day mingled with the room's dust and made me sneeze twice. Jessica, Ashley, Nikki, and Joan were dressed for something other than a poetry workshop. Adorned with trailing earrings, lip gloss, eye shadow, T-shirts with messages that exposed their bare bellies of various sizes and shapes, they had strutted rather than walked into the room. The Gang of Four, I thought. The comfort, the safety, the group.

I gave my speech then. "There are no rules," I told them. "For six weeks, three days a week, we're going to dance, dance with words. Nothing is prohibited—no thought or subject. Nonsense, stupidity, silliness of all kinds are allowed. Grammar, spelling, none of it

23

matters, at least at first. We'll read poems, but your poems don't have to be like the ones we read."

The seven were silent.

"You mean we can write about *anything*," Nikki blurted out. "Even nasty stuff."

"If that's what you want," I said. "In fact, let's try *nasty* as a trigger word."

After a short explanation about automatic writing, I had them write a response to *nasty,* whatever came into their minds in a ten-minute stretch. *Poop, pee, snot,* and *vomit* appeared under several pencils in short order. Joan included "Period mess," which prompted giggles and gasps and made me wonder how many of them had crossed that threshold. Peyton discoursed on cow pies. Emma, incapable, it seemed, of letting herself go, stuck to moldy oranges and lemons, and Alice, who obviously inhabited the realm of the incurably bookish, wrote, "sharp, cruel, pointed, like piercing knives in my soft flesh," a line that caused Nikki to roll her eyes and glance at Joan for confirmation, which quickly arrived in the form of a smirk.

That shared look of disparagement registered itself in my chest, like the briefest stab of a needle, and I noted aloud that *nasty* was a word that included more than objects of disgust, that there were nasty remarks, nasty thoughts, and nasty people. This went over without objection, and after more talk, embarrassed giggling, questions, my directive to keep their work in a single notebook, and an assignment to do more fast writing at home to the word *cold,* I dismissed them.

The Gang of Four led the way out with Peyton and Emma fast on their heels. Alice lingered at the table as she carefully, self-consciously inserted her book into a large canvas bag. Then I heard Ashley call to Alice in a bright, brittle voice, "Alice, aren't you coming with?" (*With* is a preposition allowed to hang unaccompanied by a noun or pronoun in Minnesotan.) Looking toward Alice, I saw her face change. She smiled for an instant and, gathering up her notebook from the table, ran eagerly toward the others. Alice's undisguised happiness combined with Ashley's tone had for the second time in a single hour touched a raw spot in me, more bodily than cerebral. I had been called back to a young and hopelessly serious self, a girl without the distance of irony or a gift for covering up her emotions. You ARE overly sensitive. The two tiny exchanges between girls lingered into the evening like an old and annoying melody in my mind, one I understood I had never wanted to hear again.

The girls and their blooming bodies may have been an indirect catalyst for the project I launched that same evening. It served as a methodical way to ward off the demons that arrived every night, all of them named Boris, and all of them wielding knives of various lengths. The fact that I had spent over half my life with that man did not mean that there hadn't been a period Before Boris (from now on to be designated B.B.) There had been sex, too, in that long-lost era, voluptuous, dirty, sweet, and sad. I decided to catalog my carnal adventures and misadventures in a pristine

notebook, to defile the pages with my own porno-
graphic history and to do my best to leave it
husband-free. The Others, I hoped, would take my
mind off the One.

Entry #1. Was I six or seven? I would say six,
but it isn't certain. My aunt and uncle's house in
Tidyville. My older cousin Rufus lounging on the
sofa. If I was six, he was twelve. Other family
members were around, I recall, moving in and
out of the room. It was summer. Sunlight shone
through the window, specks of dust visible, a fan
blowing from the corner. As I passed the sofa,
Rufus pulled me onto his lap, nothing unusual.
We were *cousins*. He began to rub me or, rather,
knead me between my legs as if I were dough,
and a strange warm feeling arrived, a combination
of dim arousal accompanied by a sensation of the
not-quite-right. I put my hands on his knees, gave
a push, dropped off his lap to the floor, and
wandered away. This drive-by groping must count
as my first sexual experience. I have never forgotten it. Although it was not traumatic in the least,
it was novel, a curiosity that left a definite imprint
on my memory. My view of the event, which I
never told anyone about, except Boris, surely
qualifies for what Freud (or, rather, James
Strachey) called "deferred action"—early memories that take on different meanings as a person
grows older. If I had not escaped so quickly, if I

had not been able to retain a sense of my own will, the molestation might have scarred me. Today, it would be considered criminal and, if discovered, could send a boy like Rufus to jail or into treatment for sex offenders. Rufus became a dentist who now specializes in implants. Last time I saw him, he was carrying around a magazine called *Implantology*.

Entry #2. Lucy Pumper announces to me on the school bus: "I know they have to *do* it to have children, but do they have to take off *all* of their clothes?" Lucy was Catholic—an exotic category: incense, robes, crucifixes, rosaries (all coveted)—and she had eight brothers and sisters. I bowed to her superior knowledge. I, on the other hand, looked through that particular glass darkly and had nothing to say. I was nine years old and understood perfectly that I would discover a reflection of some kind if I looked hard enough, but when I gazed ahead I had no idea what I was seeing. *All* of their clothes?

A side entry: I promised not to, but I can't help it. His hair was dark then, almost black, and there was no soft, loose flesh beneath his chin. As he sat across the table from me in the Hungarian Pastry Shop, he explained his research slowly and lucidly, and he drew a model on the napkin with his Bic pen. I leaned forward

to look at it, followed one of the lines he had
drawn with my finger, and looked up at him.
The electric air. He placed his hand over mine
and pressed my fingers into the table, but I felt
it between my legs. I felt my jaw loosen and my
mouth open. It was grand, my love, wasn't it?
Well, wasn't it?

I am screaming, All these years you came first! You,
never me! Who cleaned, did homework for hours,
slogged through the shopping? Did you? Goddamned
master of the universe! Phallic Übermensch off to a
conference. The neural correlates of consciousness! It
makes me puke!

Why are you always so angry? What happened to
your sense of humor? Why are you rewriting our
life?

> I remember pieces, parts,
> A chair without the room,
> A flying phrase, a shriek, a foggy scene,
> hippocampal fits
> that summon David Hume,
> his I as pale and lean and phantom-like
> As mine.

Dear Mom,

I'm thinking of you every day. How is Grandmother? The play closes in August and then I'll
come to visit for a whole week. I love doing
Muriel. She's a pip—a great part and finally
comedy! The laughs have been huge. I told Freddy
the scripts were awful, but he kept sending me out
for those ghastly torture-and-kill-the-girl movies.
Yuck! The playhouse is trying to raise money,
but it isn't easy here in off-off-off land. Jason is
fine except that he's hating my schedule.

I saw Dad for lunch but it didn't go so well.
Mom, I'm worrying a lot about you. Are you
okay? I love you so much.

Your own Daisy

I sent my own Daisy a reassuring message.

"He wasn't an easy man to be married to, your father,"
my mother said.

"No," I said, "I can see that."

My mother was sitting in a chair, hugging her thin
knees. I thought to myself that although age had
shrunk her, it had also intensified her, as if the lack
of remaining time had had the effect of stripping
away all fat—both physical and mental.

"Golf, the law, crosswords, martinis."

"In that order?" I smiled at her.

"Possibly." My mother sighed and reached to pick a dead leaf from a potted plant on the table beside her. "I have never told you," she said, "but when you were still small, I believe your father fell in love with someone else."

I took a breath. "He had an affair?"

My mother shook her head. "No, I don't think there was sex. His rectitude was absolute, but there was the feeling."

"He told you?"

"No. I guessed."

Such were the circuitous routes of marital life, at least between my parents. Direct confrontation, of any kind, had been extremely rare. "But he admitted it."

"No, he didn't confirm or deny it." My mother pressed her lips together. "He found it very difficult, you know, to talk to me about anything painful. He would say, 'Please, I can't. I can't.'"

As she spoke, a mental image of my father came abruptly into my head. He was sitting with his back turned to me, silently watching the fire, a book of puzzles at his feet. Then I saw him lying in the hospital bed, a long skeletal figure adrift on morphine, no longer conscious. I remembered my mother touching his face. At first, she used a single finger, as if she were drawing his features directly onto his body, a wordless outline of her husband's countenance. But then she pressed her palms against his forehead, cheeks, eyes, nose, and neck, squeezing his flesh hard like a sightless woman desperate to memorize a face. My mother, both tough and blighted, her lips pressed together, her eyes wide with urgency as she began to grasp his shoulders and arms and then his chest. I turned away from this private claim to a man, this possessive declaration of time spent, and I left the room. When I returned, my father was dead. He looked younger dead, smooth and incomprehensible. She was sitting in darkness with her hands folded in her lap. Narrow lines of light from the Venetian blinds made stripes across her forehead and cheek, and I felt awe, only awe in that instant.

In response to my silence, my mother continued. "I am telling you this now," she said, "because I sometimes wished he had risked it, had thrown himself at her. He might, of course, have run off with her, and then again, he might have tired of it . . ." She exhaled loudly, a long shuddering breath. "He returned to me, emotionally, I mean, to the degree that it was possible for him. It went on for a few years—the distance— and then I don't think he thought of her anymore, or if he did, she had lost her power."

"I see," I said. I did see. The Pause. I tried hard to remember sonnet 129. It begins, "Th'expense of spirit in a waste of shame," and then the lines about lust, "lust in action." Somewhere the words "murderous, bloody, full of blame . . ."

Enjoyed no sooner, but despised straight;

Something, something . . . then:

> Mad in pursuit, and in possession so;
> Had, having, and in quest to have, extreme;
> A bliss in proof, and proved, a very woe;
> Before, a joy proposed; behind, a dream.
>> All this the world well knows; yet none
>> knows well
>> To shun the heaven that leads men to
>> this hell.

"Who was she, Mama?"

"Does it matter?"

"No, maybe not," I lied.

"She's dead," my mother said. "She's been dead for twelve years."

That evening, as I turned the key in the lock, I felt a presence on the other side of the door, a heavy, threatening being, palpable, alive, there, standing just as I stood, its hand raised. I heard myself breathing on the step, felt the cooling night on my bare arms, heard a lone car engine start up not far away, but I didn't move. Neither did it. Stupid tears rose in my eyes. I had felt the same weighted body years ago at the bottom of the stairs at home, a waiting Echo. I counted to twenty, delayed for another twenty beats, then pushed hard at the door and turned on the light switch to face the reasonable emptiness of the mud hall. It was gone. This thing that was not a superstition or a vague apprehension, but a felt conviction. Why had it returned? Ghosts, devils, and doubles. I remembered telling Boris about the waiting presence, invisible but dense, and his eyes had lit up with interest. That was back in the days when he liked me, before his eyes went dull, before Stefan died, the little brother, who leapt and crashed, so smart, O God, the young philosopher who knocked them out at Princeton, who made them quake, who loved to talk to me, to me, not just to Boris, who read my poems, who held my hand, who was dead before he could visit me in the hospital where he had been, too, landed, too, on his flights to heaven and drops into hell. I hate you for what you did, Stefan. You knew he would find you. You must have known he would find you. And you must have known he would call me and that I would go to him. For half a second, I saw the pool of urine on the floor mixed with watery feces staining the floorboards. *No.*

Stop thinking about that. Don't think about that. Go back to the presence.

Boris had told me about presences. Karl Jaspers, *wunder Mensch,* had called the phenomenon *leibhaftige Bewusstheit* and somebody else, a Frenchman, no doubt, *hallucination du compagnon.* Had I been crazy as a girl, too? Bats for a year? No, not a whole year, months, the months of the cruelties when I had felt the Thing waiting at the bottom of the stairs. "Not necessarily crazy," Boris had said to me in his voice, thickened by cigars, and then he had smiled. Presences, he said, have been felt by patients, both in the psych ward and those in neurology, as well as by just plain folks. Yes, hordes of undiagnosed innocents, just like you, Dear Reader, whose minds are not cracked or disorderly or shredded to bits, but merely subject to a quirk or two.

I tried hard to remember then, as I lay on the sofa, presence-free, to unearth the distant cruelties of the sixth grade, "calmly and objectively," as they say on television and in bad books. There had been a plot or several plots, a grandiose word for the doings of little girls, but does the age of the perpetrators or the location of intrigue really matter? Playground or royal court? Isn't the human business the same?

How had it started? At a slumber party. Just fragments. This is certain: I didn't want to breathe in until I fainted, gulping in the air over and over to propel me forward flat onto the mattress. It was stupid, and I had been frightened by Lucy's white face.

"Don't be chicken, Mia. Come on. Come on." Whines of complicity.

No. I wouldn't do it. Why would anyone want to faint? I felt too vulnerable. I didn't like to be dizzy.

The girls whisper near me. Yes, I hear them but don't understand. My sleeping bag was blue with a plaid lining. That I remember clearly. I'm tired, so tired. There is something about an aim, aiming at someone, then aiming a knife. A cryptic joke.

I laugh with them, not wanting to be left out, and the girls laugh harder. My friend Julia laughs hardest of all. I fall asleep after that. Confused and ignorant little girl.

The note in class: "AIM, dirty fingernails and greasy red hair. Wash yourself, piglet." I saw my inverted name all at once. Mia in Aim.

"My nails are clean and so is my hair."

Gales of laughter. High winds of cackling from the group, blowing me down into a hole. Don't say anything. Pretend you hear, see nothing.

The pinch on the stairs.

"Stop pinching me."

No expression on Julia's face. "What's wrong with you? I didn't touch you. You're crazy."

More surreptitious pinches, my "imagination," in the girls' locker room.

Tears in the toilet stall.

Then, mostly, I don't exist.

To reject, exclude, ignore, excommunicate, exile, push out. The cold shoulder. The silent treatment. Solitary confinement. Time out.

In Athens, they formalized ostracism to rid themselves of those suspected of having accumulated too much power, from *ostrakon,* the word for "shard." They wrote down the names of the threats on broken pieces of crockery. *Word Shards*. The Pathan tribes in Pakistan exile renegade members, sending them into a dusty nowhere. The Apache ignore widows. They fear the paroxysms of grief and pretend those who suffer from them do not exist. Chimpanzees, lions, wolves all have forms of ostracism, forcing out one of their own, either too weak or too obstreperous to be tolerated by the group. Scientists describe this as an "innate and adaptive" method of social control. Lester the chimpanzee lusted after power above his rank, tried to hump females out of his league. He didn't know his place and, finally, was expelled. Without the others, he starved to death. The researchers found his emaciated body under a tree. The Amish call it *Meidung*. When a member breaks a law, he or she is shunned. All interactions cease, and the one they have turned against falls into destitution or worse. A man bought a car to take his sick child to a doctor, but the Amish are not allowed to drive cars. After that breach, the powers that be declared him anathema. No one recognized him. Old friends and neighbors looked through him. He no longer existed among them, and so he lost himself to himself. He cringed at the blank faces. His posture changed; he folded inward; and he found he couldn't eat. His eyes lost their focus, and when he spoke to his son, he realized he was whispering. He found a lawyer and filed suit against the elders. Not long after, his boy died. A month later, he died. *Meidung* is also known as "the slow death." Two of the elders who had approved the *Meidung* also died. There were bodies all over the stage.

It seemed to me at the time that I had fallen under an evil enchantment, the source of which could not be proven, only guessed at, because the crimes were small and mostly hidden: pinches that didn't happen, hurtful notes written by no one: "You are a big fake," the mysterious destruction of my English paper, the drawing I had left on my desk—found scribbled over— jeers and whispers, anonymous telephone calls, the silence of not being answered. We find ourselves in the faces of others, and so for a time every mirror reflected a foreigner, a despised outsider unworthy of being alive. Mia. I rescrambled it. I am. I wrote it over and over in my notebook. I am. I am Mia. Among my mother's books I found an anthology of poems and in it, John Clare's poem, "I Am."

I am: yet what I am none cares or knows
    My friends forsake me like a memory lost,
I am the self-consumer of my woes—
    They rise and vanish in oblivious host,
Like shadows in love's frenzied, stifled throes—
And yet, I am, and live—like vapors tossed

Into the nothingness of scorn and noise . . .

I had no idea what "self-consumer of my woes" meant. It might have helped. A little irony, child, a little distance, a little humor, a little indifference. Indifference was the cure, but I couldn't find it in myself. The actual cure was escape. That simple. My mother arranged it. St. John's Academy in St. Paul, a boarding school. There I was smiled upon, recognized, befriended. There I found Rita, co-conspirator with long black braids and *Mad* magazine, fan of Ella, Piaf, and Tom Lehrer. Lying each in a bunk, we crooned out in faltering harmony every verse of "Poisoning Pigeons in the Park." (I felt bad for the fictional pigeons, actually, but the sweet camaraderie of Rita far outweighed the pinch of pity.) Her pale brown legs. My white ones with a few freckles. My bad poems. Her good cartoons.

I remember my mother as she stood in the doorway to our room on the first day. She was so much younger, and I can't summon the precise features of her face as it was then. I do recall the worried but hopeful look in her eyes before she left me, and that when I hugged her I smashed my face into the shoulder of her jacket and told myself to inhale. I wanted to keep the smell of her with me—that mingled odor of loose powder and Shalimar and wool.

It is impossible to divine a story while you are living it; it is shapeless; an inchoate procession of words and things, and let us be frank: We *never* recover what was. Most of it vanishes. And yet, as I sit here at my desk and try to bring it back, that summer not so long ago, I know turns were made that affected what followed. Some of them stand out like bumps on a relief map, but then I was unable to perceive them because my view of things was lost in the undifferentiated flatness of living one moment after another. Time is not outside us, but inside. Only we live with past, present, and future, and the present is too brief to experience anyway; it is retained afterward and then it is either codified or it slips into amnesia. Consciousness is the product of delay. Sometime in early June, during the second week of my stay, I made a small turn without being aware of it, and I think it began with the secret amusements.

Abigail had arranged for me to see her handicrafts. Her apartment was smaller than my mother's and, at first glance, I felt inundated by the shelves of tiny glass figurines, the embroidered pillows and wall signs ("Home Sweet Home"), and the multicolored quilts folded over furniture. Various artworks covered most of the walls and Abigail herself, who was decked out in a long loose dress embellished with what appeared to be an alligator and other creatures. Despite the dense arrangements, the room had that neat, newly dusted, proud feeling I had come to expect from the swans of Rolling Meadows. Because she could no longer stand upright, Abigail used a walker to deftly propel herself around in the doubled-over position. She opened the door, shifted her head sideways to eye me, and, fingering her hearing aid with her free hand, looked intently in my direction. The auditory devices were not like the ones my mother wore; they were much larger and protruded from her ears like great dark flowers. Thick cords dangled from them, and I wondered whether these were extra technology for her extreme deafness or a throwback to an earlier era.

Although not nearly so big, the contraptions reminded me of ear trumpets used in the nineteenth century. She settled me into a chair, offered me cookies and a glass of milk, as if I were seven, and then, without any preliminaries, she brought forth the two works she had selected for me to examine and placed one on top of the other on my lap. Then she slowly made her way to the green sofa and carefully deposited herself in a position that was painful to look at, but her cheerful, direct expression mitigated my discomfort, and I picked up the top piece.

"That's an old one," she said. "Doesn't bother me. That's the best I can say. At least that one doesn't bother me. After I put them up, some of them get to bothering me, and then I have to put them away, go right in the closet. Well, what do you think?"

After taking out my reading glasses, I looked down at an elaborate scene of what appeared to be a cliché: In the foreground a cherubic blond boy made of felt cutouts danced with a bear against a background of riotous flower patterns. Over him was a yellow sun with a smiling face. *Happy-wappy,* I thought. The derisive expression was Bea's. But then as I continued to look, I noticed that behind the dull boy, nearly hidden by leaf patterns, was a tiny girl embroidered into fabric, her form rendered in threads of muted colors. Wielding an oversized open pair of scissors as a weapon, she grinned malevolently at a sleeping cat. Then I noticed a set of pale pink winged dentures above her that, without scrutiny, could have been mistaken for petals, and a gray-green skeleton key. As I continued to investigate the shapes in the foliage, I saw what appeared to be a pair of naked breasts in a little window and soon after some words, the letters of which were so small I had to hold them away from me to read: *O remember that my life is wind*. I knew I had read those words but couldn't place them.

When I looked up, Abigail smiled.

"It's not what it seems to be at first," I yelled in her direction. "The girl. The teeth. Where is the quote from?"

"Hollering is not helpful," she said loudly. "A firm loud voice will do the trick. Job. 'O remember that my life is wind; mine eye shall no more see good.'"

I said nothing.

"They don't see it, you know." Abigail stroked a hearing-aid cord as she tilted her head. "Most of them. They see only what they expect to see, sugar, not spice, if you comprehend my meaning. Even your mother took her time noticing them. Of course, the eyesight around these parts isn't too hot. I started doing it, oh, it was years ago, at my crafts club, made my own patterns, but it wouldn't do to come right out with it—up front—you know, so I began what I came to call the *private amusements*, little scenes within scenes, secret undies, if you understand. Take a gander at the next one. It's got a door."

I laid the small blanket on my lap and looked down at needlepoint roses, yellow and pink on a black background, with leaves in various greens. The stitching was flawless. There were also tiny pastel buttons sewn here and there into the floral motif. No door.

"One of the buttons opens, Mia," she said. Her voice shook as she spoke, and I could sense her excitement.

After fumbling with several buttons, I looked up to see Abigail grab her walker, raise herself twice before she pushed herself up off her seat, and begin to move slowly toward me—walker tap, step, tap, step. Once she had arrived, her lowered head poised just above my own, she gestured toward a yellow button. "That one. Then pull."

I pushed the button through a hole and pulled. The rose fabric gave way to a different view. The image on my lap was another needlepoint, but this one was dominated by a huge gray-blue vacuum cleaner, complete with an Electrolux label on its flank. The thing was not grounded but airborne, a flying machine guided by a disproportionately small, mostly naked woman—she wore only high heels—who sailed alongside it in the blue sky, commandeering its long hose. The household appliance was engaged in the business of sucking up a miniature town below. I studied the two legs of a tiny man that stuck out from the bottom of the attachment and the hair of another pulled upward by the air, his mouth open in terror. Cows, pigs, and chickens, a church, and a school had all been uprooted and were soon to be digested by the hungry hose. Abigail had worked hard on the suction disaster scene; each figure and building had been rendered in tiny precise stitches. Then I saw the miniature sign that said BONDEN hovering just outside the vacuum's mouth. I thought of the hours of work and the pleasure that must have pushed her forward, a secret pleasure, one touched by anger or revenge or at the very least a gleeful feeling of vicarious destruction. Many days, perhaps months, had gone into creating this "undie."

A low sound came from my throat, but I don't think she heard it. I looked at her, nodded, smiled my appreciation, and said, careful not to yell, "It's great."

Abigail slowly returned to the sofa. I waited through the taps and steps, and then through the lowering ritual that began with a double-fisted grip on the walker and concluded with a rocking drop into the seat cushion. "Did it in fifty-seven," she said. "Too much for me now. My fingers won't cooperate, the work's too fine."

"You had to hide it?"

She nodded, then smiled. "I was spitting mad at the time. Made me feel better."

Abigail did not elaborate, and I felt too much the outsider to press her. We sat together for a while without speaking. I watched the old Swan munch her cookie very neatly, gingerly wiping away a few crumbs that had settled at the corner of her mouth with an embroidered napkin. After some minutes, I said I had to go, and when she reached for her walker, I told her not to worry about showing me to the door. And then, in a fit of admiration, I leaned over, found her cheek, and kissed it warmly.

What do we know about people really? I thought. What the hell do we know about anyone?

After only a week of class, my seven girls emerged from behind their adolescent wardrobes and their tics, and I found myself interested in them. Ashley and Alice, the two *A* girls, were friends. Both were bright, had read books, even some poets, and they vied for my attention in class. Ashley was poised, however, in a way Alice was not. Alice was inward. A couple of times she absentmindedly picked her nose in class while she worked on a poem. She was inclined toward stilted Romantic images—moors, wild tears, and savage breasts—that indicated her immersion in the Brontë sisters but often sounded merely silly when she read her works aloud in emotional tones that made her compatriots writhe with embarrassment. But in spite of her pretensions, she wrote grammatically and with far more sophistication than any of the other girls and came out with a few lines I truly liked: *Silence is a good neighbor* and *I watched my sullen self walk away*. Ashley, on the other hand, had a strong sense of what would fly with the others. She liked rhymes, the influence of rap music, and impressed her friends with her agility, matching *fret* and *Internet,* for example, and *plate* with *investigate.* The girl had perfect pitch for workshop politics and dealt out praise, comfort, and delicate criticism in beneficent doses to her peers. Emma lost some of her shyness, pushed aside her hair, and revealed a sense of humor: "Never put a rainbow in a poem. Never rhyme *true* with *you*, but *scarf* and *barf* will do." After a few classes, Peyton had become so relaxed, she set herself up with an extra chair to accommodate her long legs. Like Alice's, Peyton's body lagged behind the other girls'. The hormonal onslaught of puberty showed no signs of having visited her person, and though I'm sure it worried her, I couldn't help but think that backwardness in this area had its advantages. In all events, that is how I read the grass stains on her shorts and the fact that horses, not boys, continually found their way into her poems. Jessie looked the little woman already, but I sensed she was waging an internal battle. The mature body must have come fast. The camp that welcomed it preened and smelled musky, while the other side donned roomy T-shirts to disguise ample breasts that appeared to be growing apace every week. Whatever else took place in Jessie's inner life remained hidden behind clichés. The grinding stupidity of phrases such as "You just have to believe in yourself" and "Don't let anything get you down" recurred without cease, and I soon understood that these weren't just lazy expressions but dictates of dogma, and she would not have them wrested away from her without a fight. After her early efforts, I had gently suggested she reconsider her wording and had watched her face close. "But it's *true*," she would intone. I gave in. What did it matter? I asked myself. She probably needed these slogans to end her war. Nikki and Joan remained a team, although I came to see that Nikki was the dominant of the two. One day they both arrived with chalky faces, heavy eyeliner, and black lipstick, an experiment I decided not to notice. The Halloween getup had no effect on their personas, however, which remained chirrupy. Their tittering back and forth was equaled only by the expansive delight they took in fart poems, which was mostly contagious, and they responded warmly to my short lecture on the scatological in literature. Rabelais. Swift. Beckett.

I was not deluded that I knew what was going on in the lives of these seven. After class, telephones suddenly appeared in their hands, and I watched the girls' thumbs pick out text messages at high speed, half of them, it seemed, directed at friends on the other side of the room. After a Tuesday class I found an e-mail from Ashley.

Dear Ms. Fredricksen,

I had to tell u how great the class is. My Mom said I would like it but I didn't believe her. She was right. You are really different from other teachers, like a friend. No like an ANGEL. I am learning a lot. I guess I just had to say it. Also, you have great hair.

Your very devoted Student,
Ashley

And then another message from an address I didn't recognize.

I know all about you. You're Insane, Crazy, Bonkers.

Mr. Nobody.

I felt slapped. I remembered the sign from NAMI on the wall of the hospital unit's small library: FIGHTING THE STIGMA OF MENTAL ILLNESS. *Stigmatos,* marked by a sharp instrument, the sign of a wound. Sometime much later, the fifteenth century, maybe, it also came to mean a mark of disgrace. Christ's wounds and the saints and hysterics who bled from their hands and feet. Stigmata. I wondered who would want to harass me anonymously—and to what purpose? Any number of people probably knew that I had been hospitalized, but I couldn't think who would want to send me this note. I tried to remember if I had given my e-mail to another patient, to Laurie maybe, sad, sad Laurie who had shuffled around in her slippers with her diary clutched to her chest, making small moaning sounds. It was possible, but unlikely.

As I lay in bed that night, roiled by the usual tempests—Stefan's note: *It is too hard*; the Pause shaking my hand in the lab and smiling, the memory of Boris in bed and the weight of sleep in his body, then his shrouded face as he comes out with his decision, and Daisy, tears running, the sound of her shuddering breaths and sniffs; she is sobbing about her father leaving her mother, and I think of my own inscrutable father's passion for someone else—the word *crazy* returned, and I pushed it away, and then the word in the note Ashley had capitalized, ANGEL, appeared for a moment on the screen behind my closed eyelids. I thought of Blake's celestial visitors, the legend of Rilke's supernatural gift, the first words of the *Duino Elegies,* and then of Leonard, my fellow inmate on the South Unit. He had proclaimed himself the Prophet of Nothing. He pontificated and he discoursed and he clearly loved the stentorian tones of his own bass voice, expounding to anyone who came near him. But no one listened to him, not his fellow patients, not the staff. Even his psychiatrist had looked blank as he sat across from Leonard in a meeting I glimpsed through one of the large glass windows. He interested me, however, and his grandiose appeals had genuine brilliance. On the morning of my release I had sat with him in the common area. With his balding pate surrounded by graying curls that fell near his shoulders, Leonard looked the part. He turned toward me and began his prophecies. He talked to me about Meister Eckhart as a messenger of the Nothing, who influenced Schelling, Hegel, and Heidegger. And he told me that Kierkegaard's *angst* was an encounter with Nothing, and that we lived in a time of actualized Nothingness, and this was essential and mystical; "It should not be amiss," he said, waving his index finger, "to open ourselves to the truth that Nothing is the primal ground of this world." Leonard may have been mad, but his thoughts were not nearly as addled as the powers that be in the hospital assumed. He continued his oratory by explaining that this was all related to the deeper levels of Buddhism, and as I walked toward Daisy, who had come through the door to take me home, he drifted on to Goethe's *Faust* and his descent into the realm of the Mothers and his union with the nothing, and that was the last I heard.

Lonely man. He couldn't be Mr. Nobody, could he? After I had left the hospital, I regretted that I hadn't made it clear to him that I was following at least some of his leaps, but all I could think about then was my daughter's face. That something was all that mattered.

> To recall me as she,
> rocking in rooms
> as white as eggs.
> An underground of string—
> these violent lines
> of what used to be called
> the heart, lost to
> my now-bitter mouth.
> "A tangle," he said.

No, knots.
Not this or these.
She was distinct,
I believe. Shelved.
Put her away.
Inanimate thing.
Put her away,
And let her rock.

"Dear Mia," Boris wrote. "Whatever happens between us, it is very important to me to know how you are. For Daisy's sake, too, we have to be in communication. Please send a message back when you receive this." So reasonable, I thought, such stiff prose: *in communication.* I felt like biting something. He was obviously worried. He had seen me on the day after I landed in the hospital, when I was *acute,* delusional and hallucinating, *bouffée délirante,* and I was convinced he was going to steal the apartment, push me into the street, a conspiracy cooked up with the Pause and the other scientists at the lab, and when he sat across from me in the room with Dr. P., a voice said, "Of course he hates you. Everyone hates you. You're impossible to live with." And then, "You'll end up like Stefan." I screamed, "No!" and an orderly pulled me away and they injected more Haldol, and I knew *they* were in on it.

His brother *and* his wife. Poor Boris, I could hear them say. Poor Boris, surrounded by crazy people. I remember babbling to Felicia, who had come to clean. I remember tearing down the shower curtain, explaining about the plot, yelling. I remember it perfectly, but now it's as if I were someone else, as if I'm looking at myself from afar. It all fell away after Bea arrived. But I had frightened Boris, and because he had "agitated" me on the ward, they didn't want him to visit again. I stared at the message for a long time before I wrote back: "I am not crazy anymore. I am hurt." The words seemed true, but when I tried to elaborate, all further commentary seemed merely decorative. What was there to *communicate*? And the irony that Boris wanted communication was almost too much to bear.

I don't want to talk about it. I'm waking up. Let me have my tea. We'll talk later. I can't talk about it. We've been over this a thousand times. How many times had he uttered those sentences? Repetition. Repetition, not identity. Nothing is repeated exactly, even words, because something has changed in the speaker and in the listener, because once said and then said again and again, the repetition itself alters the words. I am walking back and forth over the same floor. I am singing the same song. I am married to the same man. No, not really. How many times had he answered Stefan's calls in the middle of night? Years and years of calls and rescues and doctors and the treatise that would change philosophy forever. And then the silence. Ten years of no Stefan. He was forty-seven when he died. Boris was five years older, and once, only once, the older brother had whispered to me after two scotches that the most terrible thing was that it was a relief, too, that his own beloved brother's suicide had also been a relief. And then when his mother died—the flamboyant, complicated, self-pitying Dora—Boris was the lone survivor. His father had dropped dead of heart failure when the boys were still young. Boris did not grieve in any demonstrative way. Instead, he receded. What had my father said? "I can't. I can't." I had longed to find both men, hadn't I? My father and my husband, both prone to long disquisitions about torts or genes and so mute about their own suffering. "Your father and your husband shared a number of traits," Dr. S. had said. The past tense: shared. I looked at the message. *I am hurt*. Boris had been hurt, too. I added, "I love you. Mia."

The sex journal was not providing me with the release I had hoped for. Recording my early, furtive mastur-batory journeys up a mountain that had rather suddenly presented itself as *something to climb;* the tongue dives with M.B. that had left my mouth sore in the morning because neither I nor said youth had dared venture into territories farther south; the later, daring advances by J.Q. under bras and into jeans as he pressed on despite colonial resistance, the forces of which admittedly weakened over time, had accumu-lated a bathetic quality I found hard to ignore. Who cares? I thought. And yet, why did the mature woman look back at the girl with such coolness, such lack of sympathy? Why did the aging persona produce only expeditions into irony? Hadn't I sighed and heaved and longed and wept? Hadn't I lost my virginity in a heated but deeply confused state, still unaware, despite my adventures with M.B. and J.Q., of how exactly it all worked? I remember the wooden stairs to the second floor, the bunched sheets and blankets, but no color or details. Only that there was a dim light that shone through the window and that the branches of the tree outside moved and the light moved with them. There was some pain, but no blood and no orgasm.

The second message read simply:

Looney.
Mr. Somebody.

Although it was unsettling, I decided not to worry. These missives had a puerile ring to them, and what harm could they really do? Without an answer, the sender would tire and disappear into the nebula from which he had come. He was no more threatening than the presence behind the door—nothing but a felt absence.

From time to time my neighbors on the left, the parents of the diminutive Harpo who had turned up on my small lawn, quarreled loudly. The content of these disputes was mostly inaudible. What carried into my domain was anger: the screech of her voice that changed register when it cracked into sobs, and his booming tenor—both of which were occasionally punctuated by a crash. The crashes were frightening, and I found myself looking closely at the house and its residents. They were a young, pink, pudgy pair. I saw little of him. He drove off in the morning to some job in a Toyota and sometimes didn't return for days, a young man who must have traveled here and there for work. The young woman stayed home with her Marx brother and an infant no more than six weeks old—a person in the still floppy, stunned by visual stimuli, sucking, arm and foot waving, grunting, grimacing phase of life. How I had loved that stage in my own Daisy's path of becoming. One afternoon, while I sat outside on the rickety chaise longue that had become my reading furniture, I saw the mother through a gap in the bushes. As she held the flailing, screaming baby in her arms, she leaned over her bewigged three-year-old, deeply engaged in fierce, if controlled, negotiations about the false hair: "You can't wear it every minute. Your head must be sweating. What about your own hair? I can hardly remember what it looks like anymore." "It's not sweaty! It's not sweaty!" I put down my copy of *Repetition,* which I was reading for the sixth time, and wandered a few yards to offer my help.

My intervention meant that the fright wig remained

on the young head. The mother was Lola, Harpo was actually Flora, and the person in a paper diaper was Simon, with whom I had a conversation of coos, nods, and smiles I found extremely gratifying. The four of us ended up in the professors' yard drinking lemonade, and I discovered that Lola had attended Swedenborg College as an art major, made jewelry and sold it, that her husband, Pete, worked for a company in Minneapolis, which had been steadily cutting back its workforce, a fact Lola found "kinda scary," that he did indeed travel a lot, and that Lola was tired. She did not say she was tired, but exhaustion was written all over her soft, round twenty-six-year-old face. While we sat together, she nursed Simon with an easy, practiced air and fended off Flora's intrusions of false solicitude that threatened to unhinge her son's mouth from her nipple. I tried to distract Flora by asking her questions. At first she refused to answer me. I spoke to her back and to the wig, but after prodding and several questions, she changed character, and I became audience to a chattering, dancing, singing show-off. "Watch my feet! Look at me jump. Simon can't jump. Look, Mom. Watch me! Look, Mom!" Lola watched with a faint smile as her bald babe's eyes flickered open and shut, open and shut, his little arms reaching tremulously for nothing, before he sank back toward her breast into sleep.

* * *

Boris wrote back:

> Thank you for answering, Mia. I have a confer-
> ence in July in Sydney. Will keep you posted on
> all dates. Boris.

There was no love to my love. I gathered he hoped
to push our relations onto a civil but cold plane for
the sake of the beloved, shared offspring, and I had
a brief fantasy of bursting in on him and the Pause
in the lab, and flying from one cage to the next.
Mia, the Fury of perpetual anger, releases all the
tormented rats from their prisons and looks on with
malicious glee as their milk-white bodies shoot
across the floor.

The classes continued into the second week, and as
we eight sat around the table and wrote and talked,
I began to sense an invisible undertow among the girls
that made me uneasy. I knew that the real pull of this
force took place before and after class, during the
hours of their lives that had nothing to do with me,
and that its dynamics were part of the necessary
secrecy and alliances of early adolescence. There were
glances exchanged among them and barely discernible
nods that sometimes made me feel as if I were watching a play that was taking place behind an opaque
screen. The bits of their conversations I overheard were
stereotypical in the extreme, a primitive banter punc-

tuated by the words *like* and *so,* used chiefly to
telegraph approval and disapproval.

Like *why* do that? I mean, that's *so retarded.*

Well, isn't it? Oh my God, don't you know that's
like so uncool?

Did you see Frannie's brother? He's *so* hot!

No, dummy, he's fifteen, not sixteen.

Did you see her bag? Like it's *so* bad.

You called me a lesbian! That's sick. Oh my God.

When I listened idly to their talk during the minutes
before we began and after I had dismissed them, I often
felt the girls' speech was interchangeable, without any
individuality whatsoever, a kind of herd-speak they had
all agreed upon, with the exception of Alice, whose
diction was not infected with as many *like*s and *so*s,
and yet even she fell into the curious, moronic dialect
of Early Female. But after each child had sat down, she
became suddenly differentiated from the others, as if a
charm had been lifted and she could speak for herself.
Little by little fragments of her family story appeared,
which altered my perception of her. I discovered that
Ashley was one of five children and her parents divorced
when she was three years old; that Emma's little sister
had muscular dystrophy; and that Peyton's father lived
in California. She was going to visit him in late August,
as she did every summer. He was the parent with horses.
Alice had lived in Bonden for only two years. Before
that she lived in Chicago, and her repeated references
to that lost metropolis inevitably set off a contagion of
looks among the others. Joan and Nikki had become

fast friends in the third grade. Jessica's parents were serious Christians of some kind, perhaps of the newish variety that mingled pop psychology and religion, but I wasn't sure.

In order to scrape at their inner worlds, the ones I felt were as distinct as their stories, we began to work on the "secret me" poems. I introduced the cleft between outer perceptions and our own sense of inner reality, the misunderstandings that can sometimes shape our relations with other people, that most of us have a feeling of a hidden self, that the social self is different from the solitary self, and so on. I emphasized that this was not Truth or Dare, a game I remembered from my own youth, not an exercise in confession or betrayal of secrets we want to keep hidden. I suggested contrasting two lines: *You think I'm . . .* and *But I'm really . . .* We discussed metaphors, using an animal or thing instead of an adjective.

I praised Joan's lines.

> You think I'm bland and a little silly.
> But inside I'm a red-hot chili.

Emma compared her inner self to mud, but it was Peyton who produced the most startling image. She wrote that on the inside she was a "chipped piece of a door that looks like an island on a map." When she read this, Peyton's thin, narrow face had a pensive, taut expression. She hesitated, then explained. When she was eight, she told us, her parents had a terrible shouting fight while she was lying in bed. Her father left the house in a fury and slammed the door so hard, a part of it loosened and a chip fell off. The next morning she took the piece that had fallen and kept it. We were silent for a few seconds. Then I said that sometimes a small thing, even a bit of debris, can come to signify a whole world of feeling. "Nothing was the same after that," she said quietly.

As I walked toward the open doors after class, I noticed that Ashley and Alice were in deep conversation on the steps just outside the building. I saw Alice nod and smile, then hand over a book or notebook. After that, Ashley stepped to one side and began to type madly on her telephone. When I passed her as I left, she looked up at me and smiled. "Really good class."

"Thanks, Ashley," I said.

That night as I lay in bed, a June storm rolled in over town, and it thundered loudly, sharp cracks like a series of detonations mingled with resonant booms above me, echoing again and again. Soon after came the rushing noise of thick, fast rain outside. I remembered the great winds of my childhood, remembered waking up in the morning to see that branches had fallen all over the street. I remembered the enchanted stillness that came before the twister or tempest, as if the whole earth were holding its breath, and the eerie green color that tinged the sky. I remembered the immensity of the world.

* * *

Dr. S. said, "You sound like you're enjoying yourself."

I was shocked. How could I enjoy myself? A woman who had been abandoned by her husband and gone bananas in the bargain, however "briefly"; how could she enjoy herself?

"You seem to have struck a chord with your young poets." (I heard a chord on a guitar—metaphors often do this to me, even the deadest of the dead.) "You seem to like being with your mother. Abigail sounds very interesting. You've met the neighbors. You're writing well. You answered Boris's e-mail." She paused. "I hear it in your voice."

Feeling stubborn, I made a sound of dismissal.

Dr. S. waited.

I thought, Could she be right? Had I been clinging to an idea of wretchedness while I was secretly enjoying myself? Secret amusements. Unconscious knowledge. *There was a little girl who had a little curl, right in the middle of her forehead. When she was good, she was very, very good* . . . "You might be right."

I could hear her breathe.

"There was a storm last night," I said, "a big one. I liked it." I was rambling, but that was good, free association. "It was like listening to my own rage, but rage with real power, big, masculine, godlike, magisterial, paternal bangs in the heavens, the kind of thundering rage that makes the lackeys hop to, a baritone roar shaking the sky. I could almost feel the town move."

"You think if your anger had power, paternal power, you could shape things in your life more to your liking. Is that what you mean?"

Is that what I meant? "I don't know."

"Is it perhaps that you felt your father's emotions had power in the family, power over your mother, your sister, and you, and you were always stepping around his feelings, trying not to upset him. And you've felt the same thing in your marriage, perhaps reproduced the same story, and all the while you've gotten angrier and angrier?"

Lord, the woman is sharp, I thought. I answered her with a small, meek "Yes."

Try at another sex entry:

It started in the library with Kant. Libraries are sexual dream factories. The languor brings it on. The body must adjust its position—a leg crossed, a palm leaned upon, a back stretched—but the body is going nowhere. The reading and the looking up from one's reading brings it on; the mind leaves the book and meanders onto a thigh or an elbow, real or imagined. The gloom of the stacks brings it on with its suggestion of the hidden. The dry odor of paper and bindings and very possibly the smell of old glue bring it on. It wasn't difficult Kant: *The Critique of Practical Reason,* much easier than *Pure,* but I was twenty, and *Practical* was quite difficult enough, and he leaned over me to see which book it was. His warm breath, his beard, very close. Professor B. in his white shirt, his shoulder an inch from mine. My whole body stiffened, and I said nothing. Then he was reading in a low voice, but the only word I remember is *tutelage*. He said it slowly, enunciating each syllable, and I was his. It ended badly, as they say, whoever they are, but his eyes watching me as I undressed—*No, your blouse first. Now your skirt. Slowly*—his long fingers moving into my pubic hair, then withdrawing, teasing me, smiling, creating desperation—these wanton pleasures in the library after it had closed, these I keep safe in memory.

"George is dead," my mother said, and pressed her index finger to her mouth for a moment. "They found her this morning on the floor in the bathroom."

"Poor George," Regina said. She pursed her lips. "I doubt I'll get to one hundred and two; it's really extraordinary when you contemplate it, even for a moment."

Did people contemplate for a moment?

"Not with my leg," she continued. "I had never heard of what I have, you know. The doctor told me if I'm not careful, one day it goes right to your brain or your lungs or somewhere and you're dead, instantly." Her eyes looked moist. "If I forget the Coumadin, then, well, it's over."

"She loved to tell people her age." Abigail was steadying her hunched self with one hand on the edge of the table. She turned her head in my direction. "Never tired of it. Her oldest daughter's seventy-nine." She breathed in. "It seems another one goes every day. Alive one minute. Dead the next."

Peg examined her hands on the table. They were heavily spotted and lined with great protruding veins. "She's with her Maker." Peg had a true warble in her voice, like the throaty sound of a pigeon. "And Alvin," she added.

"Unless they've remade the man in heaven, God save her from Alvin," Abigail said forcefully. "The most persnickety little tyrant I've ever seen. His pens had to lie just so, an inch apart, his collars had to be ironed flat, flat, flat. The bed, Lord, the bed and its corners. George was lucky to be rid of him. Had twenty-seven blessed years without that bald, nasty little despot."

"Abigail, it's not right to speak like that about the dead," Peg said, her voice lilting sweetly.

Abigail was not listening. She was pressing a piece of paper into my hand under the table. I closed my hand around it and tucked into my pocket.

My mother shook her head. "I've never thought it was right to turn people into paragons of virtue after their deaths, either."

I murmured an agreement.

"Nothing wrong with looking on the bright side." Peg's voice lifted a whole octave on the penultimate word. She smiled.

"Not at all," Regina said in her oddly accented voice. "With my leg I must remain bright and hopeful. What else can I do? If it bursts, that's it, straight to my brain or my heart, dead in a second."

We were sitting in the game room, around the bridge table. The summer light came through the window and I looked out at the clouds, one of which drifted upward like a smoke ring. I heard a dryer flapping clothes somewhere down the hallway and the low sound of a motorized scooter, but that was all.

Four Swans.

Mia,
I have more to show you. Would Thursday be suitable?
    Yours,
    Abigail

Each word was a tremulous but careful scrawl of letters. I remembered what my mother had once said: "Getting old is fine. The only problem with it is that your body falls apart."

"Your poetry's cracked," my anonymous tormenter had written. "Nobody can understand it. Nobody wants twisted shit like that. Who do you think you are?!#*

Mr. Nobody."

*   *   *

I read the message several times. The more I read it, the more peculiar it became. The repetition of Nobody followed by the pseudonym, Nobody, made it sound as if he, Nobody, did understand *it* and did, in fact, want *twisted shit*. *Who do you think you are?* became another question entirely in that case. Sliding meanings. It seemed unlikely that the phantom was ironic, making some superior joke about the *novis dictum* for "accessible" poems or playing with the words *twisted shit* and *cracked*. Unless it was Leonard, released from South, and annoying me for some preposterous reason of his own. It was true that for years I had been toiling away at work few wanted or understood, that my isolation had become increasingly painful, and that I had harangued Boris with my diatribes about our shallow, debased, virulently anti-intellectual culture that worships mediocrity and despises its poets. Where was Whitman Street in New York City? I had whined about the poets who wrote for the few remaining middlebrow folk in the United States who bothered to glance at a feeble line or two in their copy of the *New Yorker* and satisfy themselves that they had just nibbled on a morsel of "sophisticated" poetic sentiment or wit about lawns or old watches or wine because, after all, it was *in* the magazine. Rejection accumulates; lodges itself like black bile in the belly, which, when spewed out, becomes a screed, the vain rantings of one redheaded lady poet against the ignoramuses and insiders and culture makers who have failed to recognize her, and poor

Boris had lived with her/my bawling ululations, Boris, a man for whom all conflict was anathema, a man for whom the raised voice, the passionate exclamation scraped like sandpaper on his soul. Paranoia chases rejection. During the days of my complete clinical derangement, hadn't I been paranoid? *They* plotted against me. Now the words on the screen, the words of Nobody, had taken the place of the accusing voices in my head. Everyone hates you. You're nothing. No wonder he left you. It was as if Mr. Nobody knew, as if he understood where to strike. I thought of George lying dead on the bathroom floor that same morning, and the future turned suddenly both vast and barren, and doubt, the deforming constant doubts that my poems were shit, a waste, that I had read my way not to knowledge but into an inscrutable oblivion, that I, not Boris, was to blame for the Pause, that my truly great work, Daisy, was behind me seemed all to be true. Now, menopausal, abandoned, bereft, and forgotten, I had nothing left. I put my head on the desk, thinking bitterly that it wasn't even my own, and wept.

After a couple of minutes of full-throated sobbing, I felt someone's warm breath on my arm and flinched. Flora and Giraffey were standing very close to me. The child's eyes were round with attention. A piece of her own light brown hair stuck out from under the wig and the skin all around her mouth had been stained pink from some unknown substance. We looked at each other. Neither of us said anything, but

I felt she was observing me with the cool eyes of a scientist, a zoologist perhaps. Her sober gaze was digesting the whole animal, pondering its behavior, and then, without a word, she acted. She lifted up Giraffey and held him out toward me. It wasn't at all obvious what she intended by the gesture so, rather than take him, I wiped my eyes with the back of my hand and patted the filthy creature on the head.

An instant later I heard Lola call her daughter loudly and urgently and, taking Flora's hand, which she accepted easily, naturally, I walked with her into the other room to greet Lola and Simon (in Snugli) outside the open screen door. I saw Lola register my face; what it looked like I have no idea—a red-gray mash of tears and mascara, probably—but her brow furrowed for a fraction of a second in sympathy. The young mother looked bedraggled at that moment, almost slovenly, in her cut-off jeans, a pink halter top, and earrings of her own making, two golden birdcages that hung from her earlobes. She had pulled her bleached hair back, and I noticed that she was a little sunburned across her nose. I remember these details because all at once I understood how glad I was to see her, and the emotion I felt has fixed the particulars of the encounter. By then it was around seven-thirty in the evening. Pete was off again and she was going to try to get the children to bed, and then, she said, with an open smile, she had a plan to break out a bottle of wine and eat the quiche she had made that day, and she would love me to join her, and I accepted with an enthusiasm that would have embarrassed me in almost any other circumstance, but which in this instance seemed entirely "normal." My mother was at her book club discussing Austen's *Emma* over a variety of cheeses, and I had no obligations of any kind.

And so that was the night we tackled the double bedtime together. On my side, this involved a complex strategy of rocking, bouncing, and occasionally shaking the just-nursed Simon, who seemed to have developed paroxysms in the gut vicinity. The little red man squirmed with discomfort, spat milk on my shoulder, and then, after straining mightily, let out in one heavenly, propulsive motion a gob of creamy yellow shit into his diaper, which I happily cleaned while examining his tiny, adorable penis and surprisingly consequential testicles and tucking up his bottom in a Pamper, and then I found a rocking chair, into which we settled, and I rocked and lullabyed the small scion of the family into the arms or, rather, the lap of Morpheus. Meanwhile, Lola waged a parallel campaign with the chattering, not-yet-four fruitcake, Flora, who dillydallied and shammed and bargained her way toward what Sir Thomas Browne once called the "Brother of Death." Valiantly, how valiantly she fought the loss of consciousness with every possible ruse: bedtime stories and glasses of water and just one more song until she, too, exhausted from the rigors of battle, collapsed, knuckle of curled index finger inside her mouth, free arm flung out across bedspread featuring

68

large purple dinosaur, while Giraffey and his companion, a peroxide beast stolen from the head of slumbering warrior, kept vigil from the bedside table.

Lola and I ate the quiche and slowly got potted over the course of several hours. She lay on the sofa, birdcages catching the light, her tanned, round legs stretched out in front of her. From time to time she wiggled her bare feet, with their slightly dirtied soles, as if she were reminding herself that they were still attached to her ankles. By eleven o'clock I had discovered that Pete was a problem, "even though I love him." Lola had been informed of my marital fiasco and a tear or two had dripped down both of our noses. We had laughed about our Problems as well, chortled loudly over their mutual propensity for odiferous socks that stiffened with some unknown manly secretion, especially in winter. The girl had a good laugh, a deep and surprising one, which seemed to come from somewhere below her lungs, and a direct way of speaking that charmed me. No indirect discourse or Kierkegaardian ironies for this daughter of Minnesota. "I wish I knew what you know," she said at one point. "I should have studied harder. Now with the kids, I don't have time." I muttered some platitude in response to this, but the fact was, the content of our conversation that night was of little importance. What mattered was that an alliance had been established between us, a felt camaraderie that we both hoped would continue. The unspoken directed the evening. When we parted we hugged and, in a fit of affection augmented by

alcohol, I cupped her round face in my hands and thanked her heartily for everything.

The transience of human feeling is nothing short of ludicrous. My mercurial fluctuations in the course of a single evening made me feel as if I had a character made of chewing gum. I had fallen into the ugly depths of self-pity, a terrain just above the even more hideous lowlands of despair. Then, easily distracted twit that I am, I had, soon after, found myself on maternal heights, where I had practically swooned with pleasure as I bobbed and fondled the borrowed homunculus next door. I had eaten well, drunk too much wine, and embraced a young woman I hardly knew. In short, I had thoroughly enjoyed myself and had every intention of doing so again.

It may come as no surprise to you that our brains are not all that different from those of our mammalian cousins the rats. My own rat man has spent his life championing a subcortical primal affective self across species, heralding our shared brain areas and neuro-chemistries. Only in later years has he begun to relate this core spot to the puzzle of higher levels of reflec-tion, mirroring, and self-consciousness—in monkeys, dolphins, elephants, human beings, and pigeons, too (most recently)—publishing papers on the various systems of this mysterious thing we call selfness, enriching his understanding with phenomenology, with quotes from the luminous Merleau-Ponty and the murkier Edmund Husserl, courtesy of HIS WIFE, who walked him through the philosophy step by step, retreating to Hegel, Kant, and Hume when needed (although the old man has less use for them, his inter-est is in *embodiment,* yes, *Leib, schéma corporel*), and read over each word carefully, painstakingly correcting errors and smoothing prose. No, you moan, not she, not she of the small stature, red curls, and comely bosom! Not the lady poet! Yes, it is so, I tell you in all gravity. The great Boris Izcovich has repeat-edly gone marauding for ideas in the brain of his own wife, has even acknowledged her contributions. So? So? you say. Isn't that all right then? It is NOT all right because THEY do not believe him. He is the Philosopher King and Man of Rat Science. After all, Dear Reader, I ask you how many men have thanked their wives for this or that service, usually at the very end of a long list of colleagues and foundations? "Without the unflagging support and inestimable patience of Muffin Pickle, my wife, as well as my children, Jimmy Junior and Topsy Pickle, this book never could have been written."

Without the bilateral prefrontal cortex of my wife, Mia Fredricksen, this book would not exist.

"That period is over," my mother said when I asked her about men in her life. "I don't want to take care of a man again." I was behind her when she said this, massaging her back, and saw only the line of her straight clipped white hair. "I miss your father," she said. "I miss our friendship, our talks. He could, after all, talk about many things, but, no, I can't see the advantages of taking up with someone now. Widowers marry again because it makes their lives easier. Widows often don't, because it makes their lives harder. Regina is an exception. I suspect she needs the attention. She flirts with everyone."

My mother, her chin lowered as I gently pressed my fingers into her neck, continued the theme of relations between the sexes with a story: Returning from her book club the night before, she had run into Oscar Busley, one of a dwindling number of Rolling's male residents. Although his peripatetic days were behind him, Oscar had retained kinesis and increased his personal velocity by means of an Electric Mobility Scooter. Busley had whirred beside my mother down the corridor, chatting amiably, as they headed in the direction of her apartment. When they reached her door, she stopped to take her keys from her bag. The man must have unclenched his fists from the Mobility's handlebars and lunged precipitously, because my mother was amazed to discover that Oscar had attached himself to her midsection. He had locked his arms firmly around her as he nestled his pate just beneath her breasts. With equal suddenness and probably greater force (she lifted weights twice a week), my mother had disengaged herself from the unwelcome embrace, rushed into her apartment, and slammed the door.

There followed a brief discussion between us about the disinhibition that sometimes occurs in cases of dementia. My mother, however, insisted that the man was "quite all right in his mind"; it was the rest of him that needed restraining. She then countered the Oscar Busley tale with the Robert Springer story. She had attended a dinner in St. Paul and met one of my father's old law acquaintances, Springer, "a tall handsome man" with "a nice head of hair," who was there with Mrs. Springer. This entirely nonviolent encounter consisted of a handshake accompanied by a meaningful gaze. By then, back rub over, my mother had moved into a chair and was facing me. She made an opening gesture with both hands, palms up. "He held it too long, you understand, just a little longer than was appropriate."

"And?" I said.

"And I nearly swooned. The pressure of his hand went right through me. I was weak in the knees. Mia, it was lovely."

Yes, I thought, the electric air.

> *. . . lift your fingers white*
> *And strip me naked, touch me light,*
> *Light, light all over.*

Lawrence in my head. Touch me light.

My mother's wrinkled, slender face looked thoughtful. Our minds moved along parallel paths. She said, "I make a point of touching my friends, you know, a pat, a hug. It's a problem. In a place like this, many people aren't touched enough."

The girls were out of sorts. It may have been the heat. We were cool inside, but outside the day was muggy—swamp weather. Alice looked especially wilted, and her large brown eyes had a rheumy glaze to them. When I asked her if she was unwell, she said her allergies were bothering her. They chattered about Facebook, and boys' names were mentioned: Andrew, Sean, Brandon, Dylan, Zack. I heard the phrase "later at the pool" several times, "bikinis," and lots of whispering and hushing. But beyond the titillating expectation of meeting members of the other sex, there was an additional tension among them, not without excitement, but that turbulence, whatever it was, had a smothered, invidious quality I could feel as surely as the humidity beyond the room. Nikki, especially, seemed discomposed. She was unable to stop herself from simpering at every possible interval. Jessie's pale blue eyes were heavy with significance, and once she mouthed a word to Emma, but I couldn't read her lips. Peyton repeatedly laid her head down on the table as if she were suffering from a sudden onset of narcolepsy. Although her expression was illegible, Ashley's always erect posture had an extra rigidity, and she applied lip gloss to her already shining mouth three times in a single hour. Emma, too, appeared preoccupied with some unknown, only half-suppressed joke. I had a powerful sensation of a text inscribed beneath it all, but I was looking at a palimpsest so thick with writings that nothing was legible.

As the class continued, I had to disguise my irritation. Nikki's pudgy face, with its sparkling eye shadow and heavy mascara, which only two days earlier had struck me as good-humored, now looked merely moronic. Joan's barely visible grin and similar makeup rankled rather than amused me. While they were writing their poems about color, I had to remind myself that some of the girls hadn't turned thirteen—that their self-control was limited and that if I allowed myself to become alienated the whole class would sour. I also knew that my hypersensitivity to the atmospheric nuances around the table, combined with my own sorry experience at their age, could easily distort my perceptions. How many times had Boris said, "Mia, you're blowing this way out of proportion," and how many times had I seen myself holding a flaccid balloon between my lips, breathing into it as it slowly expanded into a great pear or long wiener, thereby changing it from one thing into another? No, the same thing, only bigger: more air.

After a not entirely dull discussion of color and feeling—bitter, mean green; glum or soothing or huge blue; hot, yelling red; bursting yellow; blank, cold white; grumpy brown; scary, deadly black; and airy, sweet-tasting pink—they departed, and I, self-anointed adult spy, stood on the sultry front steps of the small building and watched.

There unfolded before me a kind of dance, a jostling, animated shuffle of approaches, withdrawals, and various doublings, triplings, and quadruplings. I could see, only yards away, at the end of the short block, a group of five boys, happily pounding, slapping, pushing, and tripping one another as they exclaimed, "You fuck, what'd'ya think yer doin'?" and "Get your hands off me, homo!" With a single exception—a tall boy in wide shorts and a baseball cap turned backward on his head—they were runty amours, much shorter than most of the girls, but all five—towering boy included—were engaged in what appeared to be a clumsy, testosterone-infused form of group gymnastics. Meanwhile, my seven were also in performance mode. Nikki, Joan, Emma, and Jessie shrieked with self-conscious laughter, glancing over their shoulders at their stumpy suitors. Peyton's drowsiness seemed to have lifted. I saw her aggressively insert herself between Nikki and Joan, lean down, and whisper some thought into Nikki's ear, which instantly produced in the listener another high-pitched squeal. Ashley, rod straight, breasts up, out, and forward, shook her hair onto her back with two little twists of her neck, before she moved confidingly toward Alice. The latter listened, rapt, to the former, and immediately afterward, I saw Emma glance at Ashley. It was a glittering, facetious look, but also, I realized, with a flash of discomfort, a servile one.

As they wandered off in a loose pack toward the still-raucous savages on the corner, I felt a mixture of pity and dread—pity, quite simply, because I was remembering not any particular day, or any particular boy or girl, not even the gloomy period when I was pushed out by Julia and her disciples. Rather, I remembered that time of life when most of what matters can be summed up by the phrase "the other kids," and it struck me as pitiful. The dread was more complex. In his journals, Kierkegaard writes that dread is an attraction, and he is right. Dread is a lure, and I could feel its tug, but why? What had I actually seen or heard that created this mild but definite pull in me? Perception is never passive. We are not only receivers of the world; we also actively produce it. There is a hallucinatory quality to all perception, and illusions are easy to create. Even you, Dear Reader, can easily be persuaded that a rubber arm is your own by a charming neurologist with a few tricks either up his sleeves or in the pockets of his white coat. I had to ask myself if my circumstances, my own unwanted *pause* from "real" life, my own postpsychotic state had affected me in ways I wasn't aware of and couldn't predict.

The two further amusements Abigail revealed to me that Thursday were as follows:

One floral, hand-knit tea cozy, which, when turned inside out, exposed a tapestry lining of female monsters with oozing eyes, flaming breath, breasts with spears, and long swordlike talons.

One long green table runner embroidered with white Christmas trees. When reversed and unzipped, it displayed (moving from left to right) five finely rendered female onanists on a black background. (Onan, the disgraced Biblical character, got into trouble for spilling his seed on the ground. As I examined the row of voluptuaries, I wondered if the term could apply to those of us who are seedless but egg-full. We waste those eggs like crazy, of course, flushing them out every month in days of bleeding, but then most sperm are wholly useless as well, a thought to be considered elsewhere at greater length.)

Slender sylph reclines in easy chair, strategically dandling a feather between her open legs.

Dark lady lies at edge of bed, legs in the air, two hands hidden beneath disordered petticoats.

Chunky redhead straddles the bar of a trapeze, head thrown back, mouth open in orgasmic extremity.

Grinning blonde with shower nozzle—spray stitched in neat fanning lines of blue thread.

And, finally, a white-haired woman lying in bed clad in a long nightgown, her hands pressed over the cloth against her genitals. This last character changed the work entirely. The jocularity of the four younger revelers turned suddenly poignant, and I thought about the loneliness of masturbatory consolations, of my own lonely consolations.

When I looked up from the tapestry of self-pleasuring women, Abigail's expression was both shrewd and sad. She told me she had not shown the masturbators to anyone but me. I asked her why. "Too risky" was her curt response.

It was strange how quickly I had become accustomed to the woman's jackknife posture and how little I thought about it as we talked. I noticed, however, that her hands were shaking more than when we were last together. She told me three times that no one had seen "the runner" but me, as if to be sure of my confidence. I said I would never speak of it without her permission. Abigail's sharp eyes gave me the strong impression that choosing me as a repository for her artistic secrets was not caprice. She had a reason, and she knew it. Nevertheless, she explained little and conducted a roving, shapeless conversation with me that afternoon over lemon cookies and tea, moving from her visit to New York in 1938 and her love for the Frick Collection to the fact that she was six years old when women got the vote to the poor supplies that were offered to art teachers in her day and how she had had to buy her own or deprive her pupils. I listened patiently to her, aware that despite the insignificance of what she was telling me, an urgency in her tone held me in my seat. After an hour of this, I felt she was tiring and suggested we make another date.

When we parted, Abigail grasped both my hands in hers. The squeeze she gave them was weak and tremulous. Then, lifting my hands to her lips, she kissed them, turned her head to one side, and pressed her cheek hard against the skin of my knuckles. Outside her door, I leaned against the wall in the corridor and felt tears come into my eyes, but whether they were for Abigail or for me, I had no idea.

I knew Pete was back because I heard him. Now that I had befriended Lola, I felt worse about the noise. I was sitting in the backyard on my chair after a long talk with Daisy on the telephone, my up-and-coming comedienne with the kind but overly possessive boyfriend "who wants to be with me every minute when he's not at work." She had called because she *needed* to discuss diplomacy. Daisy wanted to find the perfect way to tell him, "I need my space." When I suggested that the phrase she had just used seemed inoffensive, she moaned, "He'll *hate* that." Pete was hating something, too, but fortunately after only minutes his bellowing stopped, and the house next door went quiet. Perhaps the combatants had taken to the wordless thrusts and parries of copulation. My father had not been a yeller, Boris was not a yeller, but there can be power in silences, too, more power sometimes. The silence draws you into the mystery of the man. What goes on in there? Why don't you tell me? Are you glad or sad or mad? We must be careful, very careful with you. Your moods are our weather and we want it always to be sunny. I want to please you, Dad, to do tricks and dance and tell stories and sing songs and make you laugh. I want you to *see* me, see Mia. *Esse est percipi.* I am. It was so easy with Mama, her hands holding my face, her eyes with mine. She could roar at me, too, at my mess and disorderly ways, my crying jags and my eruptions, and then I was so sorry, and it was easy to get her back. And with Bea, too, but you were too far, and I couldn't find your eyes or, if I did find them, they turned inward and there was gloom in that mental sky. Harold Fredricksen, Attorney at Law. It was a great joke in the family that when I was four, I had recited the Lord's Prayer, "Our Father who art in Heaven, Harold be thy name." And Boris, yes, Boris, too, husband, father, father, husband. A repetition of the pull. What goes on in there? Why don't you tell me? Your silences pull me toward you but then there are clouds in your eyes. I want to ram the fortress of that gaze, blast beyond it to find you. I am the fighting Spirit of Communion. But you are afraid of being broken into, or maybe you are afraid of being eaten. The seductive Dora, glamour-puss mother weighted down by the myriad gestures and accoutrements of femininity, the sulks and coos and eyelash batting and shoulder rolling and hints and around-the-bend methods that will get her what she wants. I can hear her gold bracelets jingling. How she loved you, her bubeleh, her boychik, her darling, but there was something cloying in that love, something theatrical and selfish, and you knew it and, as soon as you were big enough, you kept her at a safe distance. Stefan knew, and he also knew that for her he came second in all things. Two boys with a father in heaven. And so it was, Boris, that we carried them, our parents, with us to each other. The Pause, too, must have them, father and mother, but I cannot think of her. I don't want to think of her.

The presence behind the door came and went. It was there, and then it wasn't there. I talked my way inside whenever I felt it, using my reason to trump the potent sensation. I continued to think of the presence as a speechless version of Mr. Nobody, a nut who sent regular messages but had shifted his tone from harassing mean guy to borderline philosopher, which again made me suspect Leonard. "Reality is immaterial, made from events, actions, potentialities. Regard these mysterious subjectivities that alter the mind-world, the Zeno effect! Relay this to Izcovich, your faithless spouse. Yours, Nobody."

Annoyed and upset by the reference to Boris, I quickly typed a response and sent it, regretting it instantly: Who are you and what do you want from me?

"I knew he had a temper when I married him," Lola said late in the afternoon while Simon dozed on her knees and Flora jumped in and out of a small turquoise blow-up pool. "But I didn't have kids then. Flora gets so scared." These three sentences seemed to float in the hot air between us, and I felt sad. I wanted to say, *But he doesn't hit anyone, right? He's not violent?* The questions that rose up sank back inside me, and I never pronounced the words. Lola was wearing a green bathing suit, sunglasses, and a baseball cap. Her body hadn't entirely lost the swollen proportions of pregnancy, and her breasts were large with milk. She was a hefty girl, but looking at her I found her attractive. I guessed it was her youth—her smooth skin, her curves, her unlined face, with its gray eyes, slightly flat nose, and full lips—no part of her had succumbed to age, no brown spots or protruding veins or wrinkles or drooping skin.

"I wonder if she'll ever take off that wig. Pete hates it. I keep telling him, who cares? She doesn't wear it to church. I think he wanted a sweet little thing . . ." Lola didn't finish. "He worries there's something wrong with her, hyperactivity or something."

Flora was engrossed in giving Giraffey a rather

violent bath. She was kneeling in the pool, bouncing him up and down as she sang, "Da, da, little Giraffey-boo. Bumba, bumba! Baby, you!" Giraffey was left floating, face down, and Flora began a new game—she lay back on her elbows and kicked vigorously enough to spray water onto my legs. "Watch, Mom! Look, Mom. Look, Mia!"

My feelings about Pete grew darker. What an idiot.

Pete's son squirmed into wakefulness. He waved his small fists in front of his face, began stretching his knees and spine, and by the time I held him only minutes later he was fully conscious, his dark eyes like seeds locked into mine. I stroked the down on his head, examined his mouth pursing and grimacing. I spoke to him and he answered me with small sounds. After a time, he turned and began to root for food, and I felt the shadow of a familiar sensation in my breasts, a bodily memory. I handed him to Lola. Once her son was comfortably nursing, she looked over at me and said, "He didn't want her at first. I got pregnant. We were already going to get married, it wasn't that. It was too soon for him." Lola leaned back in her chair. "Pete's an anxious guy. I knew that, too. He had an older sister who was born with lots of things wrong with her and really retarded. They had to put her in a home. She never learned to walk or talk or anything. She died when she was seven. Pete doesn't like to talk about it." Lola examined her nail polish. "His dad never went to see her, not once. The whole thing was really awful for his mom. You can imagine."

I could imagine. I looked up at the clouds, a dense cirrus configuration, and, as I watched a head dangling long streams of hair break away very slowly from a long attenuated neck, I realized that I had been more comfortable with the angry cipher Pete than with this new person, the young man with the dead sister.

It may have been the general emptiness of the view— corn and sky. It may have been the heat or my own quiet desperation or simply a need to fill the irremediably dull present with bluster and blabber, but when Lola asked me about life in New York, I regaled her with one story after another and listened to her laugh. I emphasized the crass, the prurient, and the outlandish. I turned the city into a nonstop carnival of poseurs, hucksters, and clowns whose pratfalls and escapades made for high entertainment. I told her about Charlie and Wayne, two poets who nearly came to blows over Ezra Pound one long-day's-journey-into-a-drunken-night but ended up in a literal pissing contest on the roof of a building in SoHo. I told her about Miriam Hunt, the aging heiress with the big bucks, little boobs, surgical face, and Hermès bags, who true to her name stalked young male scientists eager for her money by sidling up to them and breathing sweet somethings into their ears: "How much did you say the research project you're proposing would cost?" I told her about my friend Rupert, who, halfway through a sex-change operation, stopped, deciding that two-in-one was the way to go. I told her about the octogenarian billionaire I sat next to at a fundraising dinner who farted and sighed, farted and sighed, farted some more and sighed some more throughout the entire meal, as if he were home alone on the toilet. I told her about my homeless pal, Frankie, whose children, brothers, sisters, cousins, aunts, and uncles died at a rate of about two a week after contracting colorful or rare diseases, including scurvy, leprosy, dengue fever, Klinefelter's syndrome, leptospirosis, fatal familial insomnia, and Chagas disease. Indeed, Frankie's supply of relatives was so great, he forgot the names of the recent dead between our meetings on Seventh Avenue.

Lola's eyes gleamed with pleasure and interest as she listened to my tales of the cosmopolitans, all of them true but all fictions nevertheless. Shorn of intimacy and seen from a considerable distance, we are all comic characters, farcical buffoons who bumble through our lives, making fine messes as we go, but when you get close, the ridiculous quickly fades into the sordid or the tragic or the merely sad. It doesn't matter whether you are stuck in the provincial backwater of Bonden or wandering down the Champs-Élysées. The merely sad business about me was that I wanted to be admired, wanted to see myself as a shining reflection in Lola's eyes. I was no different from Flora. Watch me, Mommy! Look at me do a cartwheel, Dad! Watch Mia do verbal dances in Sheri and Allan Burda's weedy backyard embellished with one swiftly sagging kiddy pool.

* * *

That night I received a message from Boris informing me that Roger Dapp was returning from London, which meant that he was losing his temporary digs and would be moving in with the Pause. For the time being, this was *"practical."* He wanted me to know. It was only *"fair."* I took it like a woman. I wept.

You may well wonder why I wanted Boris at all, a man who tells his still-wife that he's shacking up with his new squeeze for "practical" reasons, as if this shocking new arrangement is simply a matter of New York real estate. I wondered why I wanted him myself. Had Boris left me after two years or even ten, the damage would have been considerably less. Thirty years is a long time, and a marriage acquires an ingrown, almost incestuous quality, with complex rhythms of feeling, dialogue, and associations. We had come to the point where listening to a story or anecdote at a dinner party would simultaneously prompt the same thought in our two heads, and it was simply a matter of which one of us would articulate it aloud. Our memories had also begun to mingle. Boris would swear up and down that he was the one who came upon the great blue heron standing on the doorstep of the house we rented in Maine, and I am just as certain that I saw the enormous bird alone and told him about it. There is no answer to the riddle, no documentation—just the flimsy, shifting tissue of remembering and imagining. One of us had listened to the other tell the story, had seen in his or her mind the encounter with the bird, and had created a memory from the mental images that accompanied the heard narrative. Inside and outside are easily confused. You and I. Boris and Mia. Mental overlap.

I didn't tell my mother about the new status of the Pause. It would have made it real, more real than I was willing to accept at the moment. Too bad I'm real, Flora had said. She had wanted to climb into the little house and live with her toys. Too bad I'm not a character in a book or a play, not that things go so well for most of them, but then I could be written elsewhere. I will write myself elsewhere, I thought, reinvent the story in a new light: I am better off without him. Did he ever do a domestic chore in his life besides the dishes? Did he or did he not tune you out regularly as if you were a radio? Did he not interrupt you in mid-sentence countless times as if you were an airy nothing, a Ms. Nobody, a Missing Person at the table? Are you not "still beautiful" in the words of your mother? Are you not still capable of great things?

The Fortunes and Misfortunes of the Famous Mia Fredricksen, who was Born in Bonden, and during a Life of Continu'd Variety for Threescore Years, Besides Her Childhood, Was Poetic Paramour and Mistress to Various and Sundry, Thirty Years a Wife (to Naturalist and Scoundrel), at Last Gained Riches and Renown from the Concerted Efforts of Her Pen, Liv'd Mostly Honest, and Died Impenitent.

Or: "No one knew who Fredricksen was. She rode into the village of Bonden in the summer of 2009, a quiet stranger who kept her well-oiled Colt in her saddle roll, but could use it to deadly effect when the need arose."

Or: "I distinguished her step, restlessly measuring the floor, and she frequently broke the silence by a deep inspiration, resembling a groan. She muttered detached words; the only one I could catch was the name of Boris, coupled with some wild term of endearment or suffering, and spoken as one would speak to a person present—low and earnest, and wrung from the depth of her soul." Mia as Heathcliff—a terrible, sneering corpse become ghost, who haunts a Manhattan apartment on East Seventieth Street, returning again and again to torment Izcovich and his Pause.

The whole story is in my head, isn't it? I am not so philosophically naïve as to believe that one can establish some empirical reality of THE STORY. We can't even agree on what we remember, for God's sake. We were in a taxi when the ten-year-old Daisy announced her theatrical ambitions. No, we were in the subway. Cab. Subway. Cab! The problem was that any number of Borises were IN MY HEAD. He was running around all over the place. Even if I never saw him in the flesh again, Boris as thought machinery was inevitable. How many times had he rubbed my feet while we watched a film together, patiently kneading and stroking the soles and the toes and the once-badly-broken ankle pained by arthritis? How many times had he looked up at me after I had washed his hair in the bathtub with the expression of a happy child? How many times had he embraced and rocked me after a rejection letter arrived? That was Boris, too, you see. That was Boris, too.

I arrived a couple of minutes late to class. On the steps I heard peals of laughter, shrieks, and the familiar mocking singsong sound of "Oh my Gawd!" The instant I entered the room, the girls went silent. As I approached them, I saw that all eyes were on me and that there was something lying in the middle of the table: a spotty wad. What was it? A bloody Kleenex.

"Did someone have a bloody nose?"

Silence. I looked around at their seven closed faces and a phrase I hadn't used since childhood came into my mind: *What gives?* No noses looked impaired in any way. I took hold of a still pristine part of the soiled paper between my thumb and index finger and escorted it to the wastebasket. I then asked if anyone would like to enlighten me about the "the mystery of the bloody Kleenex," while a mental image of Nancy Drew in her blue roadster zoomed by.

"We found it there," Ashley said, "when we came in, but it was so gross no one wanted to touch it. The janitor or somebody must have put it there."

I saw Jessie press her lips together hard.

"Disgusting," Emma said. "How could anybody just leave it out like that?"

Alice stared rigidly at the table.

Nikki glanced at the wastebasket and made a face. "Some people just aren't clean."

Joan nodded in eager assent. Peyton looked embarrassed.

"There are many things worse than a Kleenex with a little blood on it. Let's get to the real business of the day: nonsense."

I was armed with poems: nursery rhymes, Ogden Nash, Christopher Isherwood, Lewis Carroll, Antonin Artaud, Edward Lear, Gerard Manley Hopkins. I hoped to move their attention from wastepaper to the pleasures of subverting meaning. We all wrote. The girls appeared to have fun, and I praised Peyton's "tasty" poem.

> Oohen the goohen in mouther sway
> Licken and sticken and wulpen it im,
> I dub the doben and dub the crim.
> Luffen my muffin, foray!

Near the end of class, when Alice was reading her rather sad nonsense, "Lones in the wild ravage . . . ," Ashley began to cough, hard. She apologized, said she needed a drink, and left the room.

When class was over, they all rushed out, except Alice, who lingered. Although morose, she looked particularly pretty that day in a white T-shirt and shorts, and I walked over to her and was just about to speak when I heard someone behind me.

It turned out to be Jessie's mother, a rotund woman

in her thirties, her dark blond hair styled and sprayed. Her expression informed me instantly that she was on a mission of great seriousness. Neither Jessie's mother nor Jessie herself, it seemed, had expected *my* kind of poetry class. It had come to her attention that I had given the girls a poem by, long breath, "D. H. Lawrence." The writer's name alone, it appeared, augured peril for the heretofore-unpollinated imaginations of the Bonden flowers. When I explained that "Snake" was a poem about a man attentively watching the animal and his guilt for frightening it, her jaw locked. "We have our beliefs," she said. The woman did not look stupid. She looked dangerous. In Bonden, a rumor, a bit of gossip, even outright slander could spread with preternatural speed. I mollified her, asserting my great respect for beliefs of all kinds—an outright lie—and by the end of our conversation, I felt I had assuaged her worries. One sentence has stayed with me, however: "God is frowning on this, I tell you. He's frowning." I saw him, Mrs. Lorquat's own God the Father filling the sky, a clean-shaven chap in a suit and tie, brow furrowed, implacably stern, an utterly humorless lover of mediocrity, God as the quintessential American reviewer.

When I looked for Alice, she had disappeared.

I confess now that I had already entered into a correspondence with Mr. Nobody. In response to my inquiry as to who he was and what he wanted, he had written, "I am any one of your voices, take your pick, an oracular voice, a plebian voice, an orator-for-the-ages voice, a girl's voice, a boy's voice, a woof, a howl, a tweet. Hurtful, coddling, angry, kind, I am the voice from Nowhere come to speak to you."

I fell for it, pushed by my loneliness, a particular kind of aching mental loneliness. Boris had been my husband, but he had also been my interlocutor. We taught each other and, without him, I had no one to dance with anymore. I wrote to poet friends, but most of them were locked into the poetry world as much as most of Boris's colleagues had been neuro shut-ins. This Nobody fellow was a leaper and a twister. He hopped from Leibniz's *Monadology* to Heisenberg and Bohr in Copenhagen to Wallace Stevens almost without taking a breath and, despite his loopiness, I found myself entertained and wrote back, coming at him with counterthoughts and new spiraling arguments. He was an adamant anti-materialist, that much I gathered. He spat on physicalists, such as Daniel Dennett and Patricia Churchland, touting a post-Newtonian world that had left substance in the dust. An intellectual omnivore who seemed to have pressed himself to the limits of his own whirling brain, he wasn't well, but he was fun. When I wrote to him, I always saw a picture of Leonard. Most of us need an image, after all, a someone to see, and that was how I gave Mr. Nobody a face.

* * *

That night I dreamed I woke up in the bedroom with the Buddha on the dresser where I slept. I climbed out of bed, and although the light was dim, I noticed that the walls were wet and glistening. I reached out, touched the damp surface with my fingers, put them to my mouth, and tasted blood. Then, from the next room, I heard a child screaming. I rushed through the door, saw a bundle of white rags on the floor, and began pulling at them to unravel the cloth and uncover the child, but all I found were more and more wrappings. I woke up, breathing hard. I woke up in the room where the dream had begun, but the story did not stop. I heard screaming. Was I still asleep? No. With a racing heart, I understood that the sound was coming from next door. Good God, I thought, Pete. I threw on a robe and flew across the yard. Without knocking or ringing the bell, I ran into the house.

There was a wigless Flora, brown curls exposed, prostrate on the living room floor, shrieking. Her small face was purple with rage and her burning cheeks streamed with tears and snot as she kicked a chair with her heels and slammed her fists into the floor. Simon was emitting a series of desperate gasping wails from the bedroom upstairs and before me was Ashley. Standing only a foot or so away from Flora, she looked down at the child with blank, dead eyes, and I saw her mouth twitch once. When she understood someone had come in and, in the same moment, recognized me, I watched her expression change instantly to one of concern and helplessness. I swooped down on Flora, picked her up in my arms, and pressed her close to me. The fit didn't end, but I started talking. "It's Mia, sweetheart, Mia. What's the matter?" That was when I realized she was screaming, "I want my air! Air!"

"Where's her wig?"

Ashley looked at me. "I threw it away. It was gross."

"Get it this instant!" I growled at her.

Flora stopped writhing the minute her "air" was restored, and with the sniffing child in my arms I mounted the steps to the bedroom to rescue Simon. Telling Flora I had to put her down in order to retrieve Simon, I instructed her to hug my leg. The baby's little body was convulsing with sobs. I picked him up and began rocking him until he grew calmer. The three of us, now one three-headed body, lumbered slowly down the stairs into the living room.

The person I had first seen when I arrived had vanished. In her place was the Ashley I knew from class, a person who was relieved I had come, a person who had been overwhelmed, a person who hadn't known what to do when Flora had smeared peanut butter in her wig, a person who had wanted to pick up Simon but was afraid to leave Flora. It all made perfect sense. Weren't Lola and Pete dunderheads for leaving two children under four with a thirteen-year-old? I did not argue with her. I told her I understood. What was I to say? When I came in, I saw something in you that shocked me? I gleaned it from your eyes, your mouth? These insights do not count in social discourse; they may be true, but articulating them sounds insane. After I had settled the three of us onto the sofa, I asked Ashley to get me a bottle for Simon and sent her home.

The children were both exhausted. Simon collapsed after his food, his tiny curled hand pressed into my collarbone. Flora found a clinging spot a little lower on my body and rested her head on my abdomen. We slept.

I woke to Lola's touch. Her hand was moving over my forehead and into my hair. I heard footsteps in the front hall, the bullying or to-be-pitied Pete (depending on my mood), and felt Lola lift Simon from my arms. She smelled of liquor, and her eyes had a watery, sentimental look. I gave her a brief synopsis. All she did was smile, my Madonna of the Split-Level, in her low-necked sparkly top, her tight jeans, and her own golden earrings—two Eiffel towers swaying slightly as she looked down at me.

Dr. S. and I talked at length about Boris's housing arrangement, during which I leaked a small bucket of tears, and then I told her about the bloody Kleenex, Alice slipping away, Mrs. Lorquat's complaint, and Ashley's face. I used the sentence "I feel something is brewing" and saw witches steaming toads on their Sabbath. Dr. S. agreed that it was entirely possible that the girls were engaged in popularity politics, but the evidence of anything more sinister was, well, nonexistent. My blood dream interested her more.

Rags. The Change. No more children. The babes
next door. There is a wistful sadness when fertility
ends, a longing, not to return to the days of bleeding,
but a longing for the repetition itself, for the steady
monthly rhythms, for the invisible tug of the Moon
herself, to whom you once belonged: Diana, Ishtar,
Mardoll, Artemis, Luna, Albion, Galata—waxing
and waning—maiden, mother, crone.

In class, I found myself examining Ashley's face for
some sign of the frightening babysitter, but there was
no trace of her. The other girls were slightly with-
held, I noticed, but cooperative, and I did not have
to confiscate any phones. And Alice, Alice looked
happy, more than happy. She looked elated. I had
never seen her in a radiant state before. Her eyes
gleamed, and the poem she wrote had a jazzy tone
I would have thought was completely out of character. "I'm banging out my thoughts today / Singing
on a comet / Yelling in the clouds / Dancing on the
sun." Something has happened, I said to myself. Alice
left last, as was often the case. She stood over the
table, carefully depositing her notebook and pens
into her bag, and she hummed a few notes from an
unrecognizable tune.

"You're in a good mood."

She looked up at me and smiled; her braces shone
silver for an instant in the light from the window.

"Have you had good news?"

Alice nodded.

I looked at her young face encouragingly.

"You might find it silly," she said. "But I've had a message, a nice message, from a boy I like."

"That's not silly," I said. "I remember. I remember how nice that was."

As we walked to the door, I told her she should keep writing. She laughed. It may have been the first time I had heard her laugh. Outside, she jumped down the steps, turned to wave at me, and started to run. Farther down the block, she slowed her pace, but her joy remained visible in the added bounce she gave to her walk.

It was the title that got me thinking. *Persuasion.* My mother was reading it for her next book club with the other Swans and they had invited me, Mia, Mistress Degree, to say a few words of introduction. A story of love postponed, of love found, lost, and refound. Austen's heroine is persuaded to give HIM up. Persuasion: to influence, sway, move, induce, soft-pedal, weigh upon, cajole, convince, the work of words, mostly, words that play on weakness, on a vulnerable spot. Honeyed tongues wag as men sweet-talk women into parting their thighs, the smooth palaver that breaks down feminine resistance. Wily women urge men toward this or that crime; the cool seductress of cinema with a teeny little pearl-handled revolver in her purse. Speed-talking Rosalind Russell snaps lines at Cary

Grant in *His Girl Friday*. Love as verbal war. Scheherazade keeps on talking and stays alive one more night. The troubadours moon and croon for a lady's favor. I will win her with words and music. I will turn human anatomy into roses and stars and seas. I will dissect the Beloved's body in metaphor. I will compliment her. I will lure her with wit. "Had we but world enough, and time . . ." I will tell stories. I will stay alive one more night. Comedies end in marriage, tragedies in death. Otherwise they aren't so different. In the end, Scheherazade gets the man who wanted to kill her, but he's besotted by then. Anne Elliot gets Captain Wentworth. The wrap-up is swift. It is the getting him back that counts and the marrying, but in spirit, Austen knows, they were wed before and suffered the emptiness of separation for six long years. This story of Mia and Boris begins deep in a marriage, after years of sex and talk and fights. If it is to be a comedy, then it must fall into Stanley Cavell's territory, the comedies of repetition, of the already-married coming together again. The philosopher gives us a trenchant parenthesis: "(Can human beings change? The humor, and the sadness, of remarriage comedies can be said to result from the fact that we have no good answer to that question.)"

The Eleatics did not believe in change, in motion. When does one thing cease to be itself and become another? Diogenes walks back and forth in silence.

Can we change and stay the same? I remember. I repeat.

* * *

Dear Boris,

I am thinking of you in the bath, smoking a
cigar. I am thinking of that day your zipper
broke in Berkeley and it was summer and you
had not worn your boxer shorts and you had to
give a lecture, so you pulled out your shirttails
and hoped that no breeze would blow and
reveal Sidney to the audience of three hundred
or more, and I am thinking of time and rifts
and pauses and that you sometimes called me
Red, Curly, and Fire Head, and I called you
Ollie after your belly got a bit big and Izcovich
Without a Stitch in bed and that's all except
that Bonden isn't too bad, albeit a bit slow and
baked. I am waiting for Bea and then Daisy to
visit and Mama is good, and I've been thinking
of Stefan, too, but about the light days, the
laughs, the three Musketeers in the old apartment on Tompkins Place and that really is it.
Love, Mia

Dr. S. talked to me about magical thinking. She was
right. We cannot wish our worlds into being. Much
depends on chance, on what we can't control, on
others. She did not say that writing to Boris was a
bad idea, but then she never judged anything. That
was *her* magic.

* * *

Lola brought me earrings, two miniature Chrysler Buildings. I had told her it was my favorite building in New York City, and she had rendered it twice in delicate gold wire. Holding them up, I couldn't help thinking of the buildings in the city that had come as a pair, as twins, and a feeling of sorrow silenced me for a moment, but then I thanked her enthusiastically, tried them on, and she smiled. Looking at her smile, I realized how calm she was, how easy, how unflappable, and that these related qualities, which bordered on languor, were what drew me to her. I guessed that inside her head, the discourse that went on was also tranquil. My own head was a storehouse for multiloquy, the *flux de mots* of myriad contrarians who argued and debated and skewered one another with mordant parley and then started up all over again. Sometimes that internal babble wore me out. Lola wasn't dull, however. I had met people who bored me stiff because they seemed drained of all internal conference and deliberation (the SMUGLY STUPID) and others who, whatever their inner capacity for complex cogitations, lived in an impenetrable box, immune to dialogue (the INTELLIGENT BUT DEAD). Lola belonged to neither camp, and even though her utterances were neither original nor witty, I felt an acumen in her body that was missing from her speech. Small alterations in her facial expression, a slow movement of her fingers, or a new tension in her shoulders when I spoke to her made me aware of how intently she was listening, and she seemed to be able to listen even while she was adjusting Flora's shorts or putting a new bib on Simon. I suspect that she knew, without having to tell herself, that I admired her.

The offering of the Chrysler Buildings happened on a Saturday, if I am not confused, and I often am about days and dates, but as I remember it, Simon was asleep in a stroller, well strapped in, and Flora's wig was not on her head. She clutched it tightly in her arms at first, sucked on a thick bunch of strands after that, meditating deeply on some subject known only to her, and once abandoned it entirely to run into the bedroom and examine the professors' Buddha. All three looked exceptionally clean and shiny. They were off to visit Lola's parents in White Bear Lake. When I admired the children's outfits, Lola sighed and said, "If it will only last. I can't tell you how many times we get there and Flora's spilled grape juice and Simon's spit up and I'm slimy. I have clean clothes for them in the car."

That same day, Flora introduced me to Moki. As she told me about him, she swayed back and forth, pushed out her bottom lip, puckered both lips, rolled her head, and breathed heavily between phrases.

"He was bad today. Too loud. Too loud. And bouncy."

"Bouncy?"

Flora grinned at me, her eyes lit with excitement. "He bounced on the house. And then he flied."

"Can he fly?"

She nodded eagerly. "But he can't go fast. He flied slow like this." She demonstrated by moving her legs and arms as if she were swimming in the air.

She came very close to me and said, "He jumped on the ceiling and in the window and on a car!"

"Wow," I said.

She gabbled on about him, her mother smiling. They had to wait for Moki because he dawdled. Moki loved chocolate chip cookies, bananas, and lemonade, and he had beautiful long blond hair. He was strong, too, and could lift heavy objects, "even trucks!"

Moki lived. After they had left, I meditated for a moment on the imaginary and the real, on wish fulfillment, on fantasy, on stories we tell ourselves about ourselves. The fictive is an enormous territory, it turns out, its boundaries vague, and there is little certainty about where it begins and ends. We chart delusions through collective agreement. The man who believes he's emitting toxic rays while nobody around him seems to be the least bit affected can be safely said to be suffering from one pathology or another and put away in a locked ward. But let us say that same man's fantasy is so vivid, it affects his neighbor, who then begins to suffer from headaches and vomiting spells, and a contagious hysteria ensues, the whole town retching—isn't there some AMBIGU-ITY here? The vomit is real. I thought of the crazed women flailing and wounding themselves in the churchyard of St. Medard, their gruesome deliriums and convulsions, their hideous pleasures, their glorious subversion of EVERYTHING. And what did I think in my madness? I thought that Boris, in concert with "them," stood against me, and this was, in fact, delusion, and yet, wasn't it also a howl against the way things are for me, a cri de coeur to be truly SEEN, not buried in the clichés and mirages of other people's desires, buried up to my neck like poor Winnie. Beckett knew. Haven't *they* distorted me with my collusion? Ibsen's Nora dances the tarantella, but it has gotten out of hand. It is too fierce. Abigail hides her vacuum cleaner that sucks up the town. It is too fierce. I can see in my father's eyebrows that it is not right, in my mother's mouth that it is inappropriate, in Boris's frown that I am too loud—too forceful. I am too fierce. I am Moki. I am bouncing on the house, but I cannot fly.

I do believe that on March 23, 1998, the only person who saw Sidney was you.

Boris

When I read it, I smiled. Of course, he would know the date. His brain is a goddamned calendar. I was glad he remembered that I had pounced on the unzippered door to the little soldier himself, standing at attention the instant I gave the command. Oh Sidney, what have you gone and done now? Why AWOL now, old friend? You were never too bright, of course. Like all your brethren, you've served as little more than a moronic tool of your owner's alligator brain. But still,

I cannot help wondering, wherefore now, old pal of mine?

Soon, you are saying, we shall come to a pass or a fork in the road. There will be ACTION. There will be more than the personification of a very dear, aging penis, more than Mia's extravagant tangents onto this or that, more than presences and Nobodies and Imaginary Friends, or dead people or Pauses or men *offstage*, for heaven's sake, and one of these old ladies or girl poetesses or the mild young neighbor woman or the teetering-on-the-brink-of-four version of Harpo Marx or even wee Simon will DO something. And I promise you they will. There is a brewing, oh yes, there is some witches' stew brewing. I know because I lived it. But before I get to that, I want to tell you, Gentle Person out there, that if you are here with me now, on the page, I mean, if you have come to this paragraph, if you have not given up and sent me, Mia, flying across the room or even if you have, but you got to wondering whether something might not happen soon and picked me up again and are reading still, then I want to reach out for you and take your face in both my hands and cover you with kisses, kisses on your cheeks and chin and all over your forehead and one on the bridge of your (variously shaped) nose, because I am yours, all yours.

I just wanted you to know.

* * *

Alice did not come to class. There were only the six, and when I asked if any of them knew whether Alice was ill, Ashley volunteered that it might be allergies; she was quite allergic to any number of substances, and a titter spread among them, a minor contagion of humor, which gave me an opportunity. "Allergies are funny?" I said.

The girls went mum, and so we leapt into Stevens and Roethke and what it means to really look at something, anything, and how after a while, the thing becomes stranger and stranger, and I turned them all into phenomenologists and had them staring at pencils and erasers and my Kleenex pack and a cell phone and we wrote about looking and things and light.

After class, Ashley, Emma, Nikki, and Nikki's second incarnation, Joan, imparted the news that Alice had been a little "weird" lately and had "made a scene just yesterday because she couldn't take a joke." When I asked what the joke was, Peyton looked sheepish and moved her eyes away from mine. Jessie said in her high small voice that I should know by now that Alice "is kinda different."

I muddled forward, remarking that Alice was Alice, and I hadn't been particularly aware of any disturbing differences as such. We all had our idiosyncrasies and I ventured that she had seemed "up" during the last class (without letting on that I knew why), and she had written an amusing poem, so I was surprised that she couldn't take a joke.

Ashley was sucking on a mint or hard candy, and

I watched her mouth move as she pushed the lozenge around in her mouth, her eyes meditative. "Well, she takes meds for something about her mood, you know, cause she's a little . . ." Ashley gestured as if she were throwing balls in the air.

"I didn't know that," Peyton said loudly.

"She's got ADHD, you mean?" Nikki said.

"She didn't say what it's called; it's something . . ." Ashley said, eyes clouded.

"Half of school's on something, Ritalin or something," Peyton announced. "That's no big deal."

I saw Emma give Peyton a hard reproving look. Emma was not subtle.

Enlightenment about Alice was not forthcoming. I smiled at the little group gathered around me and said very slowly, "It may be hard to believe, but I was young once, too, and moreover, I *remember* being young. I remember being exactly your age, in fact, and I remember *jokes*, too." It was a cinematic moment, and I was fully conscious of it. I did my best to don my most all-knowing, authoritative, good-teacher-beloved-by-the-students expression, a cross between Mr. Chips and Miss Jean Brodie, and then I slapped Theodore Roethke shut, stood up, and made my exit. In the film, the camera would follow my back to the door, my high heels—sandals in reality—clipping smartly on the floorboards, and then I pause, just for a moment, and turn to look over my shoulder. The camera is now close. Only my face is visible, and on the screen, it is gigantic, perhaps twelve feet tall.

I beam out at you, the audience, turn again, and the door shuts with a loud Foley click behind me.

Something seemed to be wrong with Abigail. My mother was sitting beside her on the sofa, stroking her back. Regina was making noises: high-pitched, staccato wails.

"She fell," Mama said to me, her face white. "Just now."

Abigail was examining her knees with a confused expression, and I felt a spasm of fear. I bent over her, took her hand, and asked all the usual questions, beginning with "Are you okay?" and moving on to particulars about pains and odd sensations. She didn't answer but stared hard downward and then began shaking her head slowly.

Regina flapped her hands in the air and in a strangled voice said, "I'm going to pull the string for help right now. I'm going into the bathroom to yank it. She can't talk. Oh my God. I have to call Nigel. He'll know what to do." (Nigel was the Englishman, and exactly what he was going to do in Leeds for Abigail in Bonden was a secret known only to Regina.)

Abigail turned her head toward her panicked friend and said in a loud even voice, "Shut up, Regina. Someone help me adjust my bra before it chokes me."

Regina looked offended. She folded her hands and sank back on the sofa, a ladylike frown on her still remarkably pretty face.

Together, my mother and I managed to pull down the offending garment, which had slipped upward in the excitement, and settle our mutual friend on the sofa.

"Abigail," my mother said. "I was so scared."

Falling was a universal fear at Rolling Meadows. Some people, like George, never got up. Hips snapped, ankles cracked, and they were never the same. Old bones. That Abigail had not broken some piece of her frail skeleton struck me as supernatural. I discovered later that my mother, perhaps unwisely, had intervened with her own body and turned a crash into a slow tumble.

At some point during the conversation that followed, I understood that Abigail felt considerably better, because she began to signal me with her eyebrows, a gesture followed by peering down at her lap. I had no idea what she was up to until I saw that she had her hands in the pockets of her embroidered dress and was exposing small parts of their red linings. The woman was *wearing* a secret amusement. Concealed inside her pockets was some subversive message, erotic needlepoint, or other undie, no doubt created years ago. I telegraphed back my silent comprehension that the dress was loaded, so to speak, another hidden fabric in Abigail's private arsenal, and this tacit knowledge between us appeared to give her genuine pleasure, because she smiled slyly and gave me some extra eyebrow lifts to confirm our complicity. Peg arrived then and, after hearing the story, took it in the vein most true to her nature, declaring Abigail "blessed" and my mother a "hero" (a designation my mother adamantly disavowed, but which she clearly enjoyed), and then she moved on to Robin Womack, a local television personality with abundant hair. She ended her eulogy with the phrase "He can put his shoes on my bed anytime!" Although I found the reference to shoes superfluous, this permission clearly imparted a fancy for Womack and his serious hair.

Exactly how we arrived at poetry I am not certain, but the Swans fondly recalled some loved lines from their earlier days. Peg wandered lonely as a cloud, and my mother read aloud Wallace Stevens's "The Reader." There are no words on his reader's page, only "the trace of burning stars / In the frosty heaven." And Regina recalled Joyce Kilmer's immortal American "tree," and I recited Ron Padgett's poem "Haiku." "*That* was fast. / I mean life." I had always laughed aloud at that poem, but not one of the Swans emitted even the briefest chuckle or snort. My mother smiled sadly. Abigail nodded. Peg's eyes glazed over with what I guessed were memories. Regina appeared to be on the verge of tears, but then she hoped aloud that I hadn't given my girls "that poem," to which I responded that it would be entirely lost on them because at their age life truly is long. Time is a question of both percentages and belief. If half your life ago you were six or seven, the span of those years is even longer than fifty for a centagenarian, because the young experience the future as endless and normally think of adults as members of another species. Only the aged have access to life's brevity.

Regina then informed me, in a muddled speech of frustrating vagueness, that something had "happened" to one of the girls in my class. She simply couldn't remember the name of the child, "Lucy perhaps, no, Janet, no, not that either," but whatever the girl's name was, Regina had heard from Adrian Bortwaffle's brother-in-law, who was a close friend of Tony Rosterhaus's (Tony's connection to my class was completely unknown to me and to Regina), that there had been an accident of some kind, and the girl had spent a night in the hospital.

There are times when the fragility of all living things is so apparent that one begins to wait for a shock, a fall, or a break at any moment. I had been in this state since Boris left me and my nerves exploded—no, earlier than that, since Stefan's suicide. There is no future without a past because what is to be cannot be imagined except as a form of repetition. I had begun to expect calamities.

My mother and I walked Abigail to her apartment and then helped her get comfortable on her sofa. She ordered us several times to "stop fussing," but in her face I read relief that she was not alone, not alone yet. She promised to see her doctor and kissed us both before we left.

Later that evening, I saw the multicolored bruise my mother had sustained on her side when she rescued her friend from the floor. The walker had somehow been involved and my mother must have banged into it hard. "You mustn't mention it to Abigail," my mother said. She said it several times. I promised several times. We sat together in the living room and I felt the hush of the building, nearly silent except for the sound of a distant television.

"Mia," she said, not long before I left her. "I want you to know that I would do it all over again."

My mother sometimes behaved as if I had access to her thoughts. "What, Mama?"

She looked surprised. "Marry your father."

"Despite your differences, you mean?"

"Yes, it would have been nice if he had been a little different, but he wasn't, and there were so many good days along with the bad days and sometimes the very thing I wanted to change about him one day was the thing that made another thing possible another day that was good, not bad, if you see what I mean."

"Such as?"

"His sense of duty, honor, rectitude. What made me want to scream one day could make me proud the next."

"Yes," I said. "I understand."

"I want you to know how good it's been to have you close, how happy I've been. I've had fun. It can be rather lonely here and you have been my happiness, my comfort, my friend."

This rather formal little speech made me glad, but I recognized in the hint of ceremony the ever-present pinch of time. My mother was old. Tomorrow she might fall or be stricken suddenly. Tomorrow she might be dead. When we parted at the door, my small mother was wearing flowered cotton pajamas. The pants ballooned around her tiny thighs and stopped just above the knobs of her scrawny anklebones. She was holding a liver-colored hot water bottle in her arms.

Daisy wrote:

Dear Mom,

I saw Dad for lunch and he didn't look so good. He had stains all over his shirt, smelled like an ashtray, and he hadn't shaved. I mean, I know he often waits a couple days, but he looked like he hadn't shaved in a week, and even worse, I thought he might have been crying before he saw me. I told him he looked bad, like a clochard, but he just kept saying he was fine. I'm fine. I'm fine. Mr. Denial. Any thoughts? Should I keep trying to get him to talk to me? Send out a detective? It won't be long now, Mamasita, before I see you!

Big kisses from your own Dazed-and-still-disappointed-in-Daddy Daisy.

* * *

I replied:

> Your father couldn't have been crying. He only
> cries at the movies. But do check on him.
>
> Love, Mom

I had known Boris for perhaps a week when he took
me to Elia Kazan's *A Tree Grows in Brooklyn* at the
Thalia on Ninety-fifth and Broadway. There is a
moment in the film when the young heroine, played
by Peggy Ann Garner, walks into a barbershop to
retrieve her dead father's shaving mug. It is an affect-
ing scene. The girl adored her drunken, sentimental
father, with his false hopes and impractical dreams,
and losing him is a massive blow. I don't believe Boris
sniffed, although he may have, but for some reason,
I turned to look at him. The man beside me oozed
tears in two heavy streams as the liquid dripped
steadily off his chin and onto his shirt. I was so astonished by this display of feeling, I politely ignored it.
Later, I came to understand that Boris responded far
more directly to the indirect; that is to say, his real
emotions surfaced only when mediated by the unreal.
Time and again, I had sat dry-eyed beside him while
he snuffled and wept over actors on a big, flat screen.
I had never, ever seen him cry in the so-called real
world, not for Stefan, not for his mother, not for me
or for Daisy or for dead friends or for any human

being who wasn't made of celluloid. That said, I was shaken by the oddly frightening thought that Boris had changed, that if he hadn't met Daisy immediately after a movie (which seemed unlikely since he worked all the time and had mostly watched films on DVD in recent years) the Pause might have altered the deep structure of Boris's character. Was he crying over her, the Frenchwoman searching for new neuropeptides? Had the wall come down for her?

Nobody was on the rampage. Nobody understood Nobody—that was the gist of the problem. The two of us had stumbled onto "the hard problem": consciousness. What is it? Why do we have it? My highly conscious correspondent inveighed against the monumental stupidities of scientism and the atomization of processes that were clearly inseparable, "a flow, flood, wave, stream, not a series of rigid discrete pebbles lined up in a row! Any idiot should be able to divine this truth. Read your William James, that stupendous Melancholic!" A Thomas Bernhard of philosophy, Nobody indulged in splenetic rages that had a weirdly calming effect on me. I loved the Stupendous Melancholic, too, but I steered him to Plutarch's flux and flow, the Greek wit who railed against the Stoics in his *On Common Conceptions:*

1) All individual substances are in flux and motion, letting go parts of themselves and receiving others coming from elsewhere.
2) The numbers and quantities to which they come or from which they go do not remain the same but become different, as the substance accepts a transformation with the said comings and goings.
3) It is wrong that it has become prevalent through custom that these changes are called growth and diminution. It would be appropriate that they should instead be called creation and destruction (*phthorai*), because they oust a thing

from its established character into a different one, whereas growth and diminution happen to a body that underlies the change and remains throughout it.

The story is old. When does one thing become another? How can we tell? He attacked Boris, too, as a naïf, a man whose notions of a sub or primal self were absurd, misplaced. "You can't locate the self in neural networks!" I defended my alienated family member with some vigor, arguing that self was an elastic term certainly, but Boris was quite specific about what he meant—that he was talking about an underlying biological system necessary for a self. According to my invisible comrade, not only Boris but everybody was asking the wrong questions, with the exception of Nobody himself, isolated spokesman for a synthetic vision that would unite all fields, end expert culture, and return thought to "dance and play." A utopian nihilist is what he was, a utopian nihilist in a manic phase. I kept thinking what he really needed was a good, long head rub. And yet, I did say to myself, When I was mad, was I myself or not myself? When does one person become another?

Do you remember, I wrote to Boris, *that evening two years ago when we realized we had just had exactly the same thought, not an obvious one at all, a rather eccentric notion that was brought about by some mutual catalyst, and you said to me,* "You know, if we lived together another hundred years we would become the same person?" *Ton amie, Mia*

When Alice didn't show up in class and I asked for information, the girls played dumb, or at least, that is what I guessed. I didn't know whether the hospital rumor was true, and it seemed silly to perpetuate it, so I went to the source. I called Alice's house, her mother answered, and she told me that Alice had been ill with severe stomach pains and had been rushed to the hospital, but the doctors had found nothing and had sent her home after a night of tests. When I asked how her daughter was feeling, she said she seemed to be out of pain but was listless and low and refused to go back to class. With all the delicacy I could muster I said that there had been talk about "a joke" on Alice among the girls, and it had worried me. I wanted to speak to Alice. The woman was obliging, even eager, I thought, and I heard in her voice that particular note of maternal fear founded not on evidence but on a feeling.

Alice did not get up for me. I was ushered into her abnormally neat pale blue room, where she lay on top of her pale blue bedspread covered with white cumulus clouds and stared at the ceiling, her arms crossed over her chest like a corpse that had been prepared for burial. I pulled a chair near her bed, sat down on it, and listened as her mother discreetly pulled the door shut behind her. The girl's face was masklike. As I spoke to her, she didn't move a muscle. I told her we had missed her in class, that it wasn't the same without her, that I was sorry she had been ill but hoped she would return soon, once she was fully recovered.

Without turning her head to look at me, she said to the ceiling, "I can't go back."

Not telling is as interesting as telling, I have found. Why speech, that short verbal journey from inside to outside, can be so excruciating under certain circumstances is fascinating. I pressed her, kindly, but I pressed. All Alice did was shake her head back and forth. I mentioned "the joke" then, and her face broke into an expression of pain. Her lips disappeared as she curled them inward, and I saw a tear dribble from each duct, and because she was supine, neither fell. Rather, they sank into the skin of her cheeks.

We are going to leave Alice lying there on her cloudy bedspread with her shiny cheeks. We are going to take a respite, because, although I remained sitting there in person, I left myself for at least half an hour. I took a mind walk. It is not easy talking to a thirteen-year-old who does not want to talk to you or, if she does want to talk to you, must nevertheless be coddled and coaxed and wheedled for the few precious utterances that will resolve the mystery of the crime. To be frank, it's a bit boring, so we shall dispense with the long and tortured job of getting the words out of the child and return to her once she has produced them.

*   *   *

Why I thought of that erotic explosion I can't say. The clouds, the bed, the light that shone through the girl's window that afternoon, a thick haze of summer illumination—any or all may have done it. Boris had accompanied me to a poetry festival, where I had read to a crowd of twenty (quite good, I thought) and we had wandered about San Francisco in the foggy air. A fellow poet had recommended a massage therapist, a man of sterling quality who altered human bodies with his hands. This was an attractive idea for someone whose crammed and speeding head occasionally lost sight of her body far below. The man's name was Bedgood. Archibald Bedgood. I am not a liar. It may have been his name that started the whole enterprise. Nothing is certain. Anyway, while Boris waited in the wings (a restful room with New Age music designed to turn all human beings into somnambulists), I lay myself down naked but for a towel covering my rump on Bedgood's massage bed, with some anxiety, if the truth be told, and the man began to rub. He was methodical, decorous—by some magic the towel never lost its purpose as modest covering. He took each body part individually, all four limbs, feet and hands, back and head, even my face at the end. I had no sexual feelings whatsoever, no erotic leaps or fantasies. I had no thoughts that I recall, but after an hour and a half, Bedgood had reduced me to jelly. Mia was missing, missing in action, so to speak. The person who emerged from the massage room to find Boris snoring on a soft pink sofa had been transformed, just as advertised. She had been remade into a limp, empty-headed, but altogether euphoric being. After rousing Izcovich from his pastel divan, this redone personage (who deserved a new name: FiFi or Didi or Dollface or just Doll) sauntered arm in arm with Husband toward Poetry Hotel, and that is where on the somewhat too soft bed I (or she) was split open, broken into flaming pieces, and transported to Paradise four times in quick succession.

The experience deserves commentary, not a word of which forwards any conventional notion of Romance. Post Bedgood ministrations, any person—no, I amend that—any person, bird, beast, or even inanimate object (provided it wasn't cold) could have sent me flying into the higher regions of erotic experience. The lesson here is that extreme relaxation promotes pleasure and extreme relaxation is a state of nearly complete openness to whatever comes along. It is also thoughtlessness. I began to wonder whether there were people who lived their lives loose, easy, and fairly blank much of the time, whether there were Dollfaces out there in a kind of permanent sensual transport. I once read about a woman who had regular orgasms brushing her teeth, a report that astonished me, but which after Bedgood began to make some sense. A toothbrush might have done it.

Only a couple of years ago at a discussion group on sex and the brain, I was SHOCKED when a colleague of Boris's assured me that in the animal kingdom—or, rather, in the female side of the animal kingdom, in other words, in the whole animal queendom—only human women experience orgasm. When I expressed my amazement, Boris and five other male researchers at the table concurred with Dr. Brooder. We two-leggers could do it but no other animals. In males, of course, prowess went all the way down the mammalian ladder. Male arousal has deep biological roots; in women it's just a fluke, an accident. From a purely physiological point of view, this struck me as absurd. My primate sisters, who shared so much of my equipment, upstairs and downstairs, had no fun during sex! What did that mean? Among our four-legged cousins, only the males experienced joy? While I argued my point, Boris glowered at me from across the table (I had been admitted as a special guest). A couple of books and several papers later, I discovered that the smug six were dead wrong, which meant, of course, that I was dead right. In 1971 Frances Burton verified orgasm in four out of five of the female rhesus monkeys in her lab. Female stump-tailed macaque monkeys experience orgasms regularly but most often with other females, not with males, and when they come, the simian ladies cry out just as we do. Alan F. Dixson, the author of *Primate Sexuality: Comparative Studies of Prosimians, Monkeys, Apes, and Human Beings,* writes that they express their rapture in sounds reminiscent of Mrs. Claus: "Ho, ho, ho!" I used those three verbal ejaculations when I confronted the old man with my evidence. "Ho! Ho! Ho!" I said, slapping down two tomes and six articles, all marked with Post-its.

Why, you may ask, did the no-fun theory for girl apes become so well known that all six guys at the table had swallowed it as a matter of course, even though the primates in question have clitorises, as do ALL female mammals? Onan, if you recall from page 77, was punished for wasting his seed. He was supposed not to cast it on the ground but to put it somewhere—inside a woman. This is the waste-not-want-not-for-children argument. But unlike Onan, who can't inseminate anybody without orgasm, Onan's hypothetical woman (the woman he should have been inside) can conceive without having the big O, a fact recognized by Aristotle but forgotten for centuries. In 1559 Columbus discovered the clitoris (*dulcedo amoris*)—Renaldus Columbus, that is. He sailed into it during one of his anatomical voyages, although Gabriele Fallopius disputed this, insisting that he had seen the hillock first. Permit me to draw an analogy between the two exploring Columbuses, Christopher and Renaldus. Their disclosures, less than a hundred years apart, the former of a body of land, the latter of a body part, share a familiar hubris, one of hierarchical perspective. In the case of the new world, the viewer looking down is European. In the clitoral case, he is a man. Both the peoples who had been living on "New World" soil for thousands of years and, I dare say, most women would have been stupefied by these "discoveries." That said, the clitoris remains a Darwinian puzzle. If it's not needed for conception, WHY is it there? Is it adaptive or nonadaptive? The shriveled-up little penis (nonadaptive) view has a long history. Gould and Lewontin argue that clits are like tits in men, an anatomical leftover. Others say no; the pleasure pea serves an evolutionary purpose. The battles are bloody. But, I ask you, what matters adaptation or size if the blessed little member does the job? Before we return to our story, I leave you with the immortal words of Jane Sharp, a seventeenth-century Englishwoman and practicing midwife, who wrote of the clitoris, "It will stand and fall as a yard doth and makes women lustful and take delight in copulation." (Women, I contend, their simian sisters, and, awaiting further research, probably other mammals, too. Further subcommentary: Doesn't the seventeenth-century use of the measurement *yard* for penis strike you as a bit of an exaggeration, unless the yard then was not the yard now?)

When Columbus spied the Mount of bliss,
He stopped and asked himself, "What is this?"
A button, a pea?
An anomaly?
No, silly man, it's a clitoris!

Alice's confession was not coherent, but it was possible to piece together a narrative after it was over. She spoke to me and to her mother, Ellen, who was admitted not long after the bean-spilling began. My eyes moved from child to mother as the girl shifted from barely audible whispers to choked admissions to hoarse gasping sobs. I noted that the mother's face functioned as a vague mirror of her child's. When Alice spoke softly, Ellen leaned forward, her eyes intent as her lips registered every insult with tiny movements. When Alice cried, Ellen's eyes grew smaller, a wrinkle appeared between her brows, and her mouth tensed into a thin straight line, but she did not weep. Maternal listening is of a special kind. The mother must listen, and she must empathize, but she cannot identify entirely with the child. This calls for an enforced remove, a distance acquired only by steeling oneself against the story being told. The knowledge *they have hurt my child* can easily summon a brute response, something on the order of *I will tear those little tarts into a thousand pieces and gobble them up for dessert*. Watching Ellen, I sensed that she was resisting the desire for grisly vengeance, and I realized that I liked her—both for her rage and for blocking it.

Alice had been receiving ugly messages for quite some time. "Skank" and "Ho" had appeared regularly as text messages, as had the highly original commentaries "You think you're so smart," "Go back to Chicago if it's so great there," "Ugly slut," "skinny weird bitch," and "Fake." All anonymous. As for my cabal of girl poets, Alice admitted that they had been on again and off again with her, one day confiding, the next, cold. They reeled her in and they cast her out. When, after weeks of misery, she confronted them with the bald statement "What did I do?" they snickered, rolled their eyes, and chanted "What did I do?" over and over again. It pained me especially to think of Peyton among the tormenters. Then photos of a naked Alice standing in front of her own mirror at home had been posted on Facebook—blurry images taken with the spy's cell phone through a crack in the blind. The poor kid snuffled hard when she coughed up this humiliation. She had taken the pictures down, of course, but not before the damage had been done. The memory of my changing body at thirteen and the achingly private, protective feeling I had had for my newly swollen breasts, three pubic hairs, and the mysterious red lines that appeared on my hips (which I discovered only two years later were stretch marks) made me squirm with discomfort. The bloody tissue narrative was garbled, but eventually Ellen and I understood that Alice had gotten her period just before my class and had been unequipped and too shy to ask any of her "friends" for a pad. She had stuffed her underpants with the Kleenex she was carrying in her purse (always on hand for her allergies), but when she walked into the room, one slightly bloody tissue had dislodged itself from her shorts and fallen to the floor, at which moment Ashley had grabbed it and then, pretending to understand all at once what she had touched, had thrown it on the table and begun to squeal the word *gross*. The most recent ruse, the one that must have induced the stomach pains, involved the message from the desired boy, Zack, who had arranged to meet her at the park near the swings at three. That must have been where Alice was off to when I saw her bouncing down the sidewalk after she left class at two forty-five. Upon her arrival, however, there was no Zack. She waited half an hour and then, realizing that something was wrong, sat down on the grass, put her hands over her face, and cried. When the tears came, so did the jeers and laughter from behind a tall fence that bordered the park. The invisible hooting girls berated Alice for her fantasy that a boy like Zack would even look at her. This was, it seemed, the most recent "joke," the one Alice hadn't been able to "take."

Despite its particulars, Alice's story is depressingly familiar. Its basic structure is repeated, with multiple variations, everywhere all the time. Although occasionally overt, the cruelties are most often hidden, surreptitious jabs to shame and hurt the victim, a strategy most often adopted by girls, not boys, who go for the direct punch, blow, or kick in the groin. The duel at dawn, with its elaborate legalisms, its seconds and its paces; its mythical reincarnation in the Wild West when black hat and white hat face off with their six-shooters; the plain old let's-take-it-outside fisticuffs between two male disputants, who are each cheered on by a rooting faction; even the playground brawl (young boy returns home beaten bloody to face Father, who says, "Son, did you win?")—all are granted a dignity in the culture that no female form of rivalry can match. A physical fight between girls or women is a catfight, one characterized by scratching, biting, slapping, flying skirts, and a scent of the ridiculous or, conversely, of erotic spectacle for male enjoyment, the delectable vision of two women "going at it." There is nothing noble about emerging victorious from such a squabble. There is no such thing as a good, clean catfight. As I sat there looking at Alice's sad, red countenance, I imagined her socking Ashley in the jaw and wondered if the masculine solution wasn't more efficient. If girls banged each other over the head instead of plotting nasty little games of sabotage, would they suffer less? But that, I thought, could only happen in another world. And even in that improbable world where a girl could dust herself off after a wrestling match with her nemesis and declare victory, what good would it do?

By the time I said good-bye to them, Ellen had managed to coax her big girl onto her lap. Mother and daughter were enfolded in the beanbag chair, where Ellen had been sitting alone only minutes before, listening to Alice's saga of intrigue and deception. Alice buried her head in her mother's neck, and her long bare legs and feet hung over the side of the chair. Ellen's hand was moving up and down her daughter's back, slowly and rhythmically. Behind the two, I noticed a row of the child's dolls on a shelf. The impassive porcelain face of one of them stared at the wall behind me. Another poppet had a faint smile on her pink lips. A woman doll in a kimono stood rigidly at attention. An antique baby lay on her back with her arms in the air. The chorus, I said to myself, and they began to stir and move their lips in unison. I saw their teeth. The old magic trembled inside them all for an instant, *animus, élan vital*. On the sidewalk as I made my way "home," I had a wild thought:

> *But I can no longer stand in awe of this,*
> *Nor, seeing what I see, keep back my tears.*

As my feet moved, one in front of the other, my gait jogged loose the source. It had arrived courtesy of the doll chorus. *Antigone*. I smiled. A tragedy for a travesty, but still, I said to myself, there is grief. And who is to measure suffering? Which one of you will calculate the magnitude of pain to be found inside a human being at any given moment?

> Multiply by words, Alice—
> Your airborne army spits spears,
> Cracks syllables, breaks glass
> Spews fury skyward.
> The hundred tricksters
> In flight on the page are you,
> A swarm of grins penciled in
> While oval heads are trampled underfoot,
> Or name the Gorgon in the mirror
> Alice. The monster twin, the other story,
> Whose mouth blasts killing winds,
> Forbidden thoughts, brazen phrases
> Held back in the years of silent sainthood.
> Good behavior. Conduct E for excellent.
> Weep, Alice, if you want to, howl!

Make it rain, a deluge
Of N's for needles from your eyes.
Your many I's. Your multitudes.
Be foment, Alice, ruckus, tirade, trouble,
And if you wish, wish three times.
Wish them out. Write them null.
Blacken their bodies with ink.
Gorge them on sublimated sweets
Until they reel and fall
Beneath your dancing feet.

I wasn't at all sure I liked the poem, but it felt awfully good to write it. "Why are they so mean to me?" Alice had uttered this several times in a soft, bewildered voice. Wasn't this the puzzled refrain of the "kinda different?" Jessie had said that by now I ought to know that Alice was "kinda different." How different? Perception is laden with visible differences, with light and shadow and object masses and moving bodies, but also always there are invisible differences and similarities, ideas that draw the lines, separate, isolate, identify. I was, am kinda different. Not one of the gang. Outside, always outside. I feel the cold winds blow over me. I would have to decide what to do about them: the clique, the girls. I couldn't let the business go. But I would have to resist hating them, my six still unformed little broads with their sadistic pleasures, the envy they sweated from their pores, and their shocking lack of empathy. Ashley, the princess of punishment.

Hadn't I seen it when she looked at Flora? Ashley, my devoted student. The girl wanted power. No doubt she had too little at home, a middle child in that large family who had probably fought for recognition from Ma and Da. Look at me! Surely, she deserved sympathy, too. I thought of her mother; it is worse to be the mother of a bully than a victim, worse to have a cruel child than one whose vulnerability allows attack. I would have to devise a strategy, if not to save the situation, at least to bring it into the open air. I like that expression, the open air. Before me I see the wide fields outside Bonden, flat and broad, with the immense sky over them.

I cried on Bea the first night after she arrived. You'd think that all the bawling and blubbering I had done over the course of about six months would have drained my ducts and left my eyeballs permanently damaged from flooding, but it seems that there is an endless supply of the salty secretion, and it can pour forth at regular, bounteous intervals without any lasting effects. The old fleshy temple truly is a marvel. It felt so good to have Bea patting my back and shushing me and rocking me a little in her arms. Mia and Be-a. Once we had dispensed with my keening lachrymosity, we settled into the Burdas' bed, and she filled me in on the doings of Jack and the boys. (Jack, the same old, same old, driving her crazy with his weekend sculpting, the results of which she referred to as *erections* because they were, each and every one, towering protrusions inspired by the Gaudí phalluses on top of the Padrera, but she did *not* want them all over the lawn. She did not want a skyline of yards in the yard, for Christ's sake. Jonah thriving in college, Ben a little lost in class but soaring in musical theater and no girlfriend ever, and *maybe he's gay,* which was fine by Bea, she just knew she couldn't say it first, what kind of mother would do that, if he was or wasn't, and then he had never been obviously *fey,* or anything like that, so they'd just have to let him figure it out, and her lawyering, which she loved the way Harold had, Our Father before her, the subtleties and loop-holes and the precedents and even the grind.)

And then with our two heads, one brown, one red, propped on pillows, we lay beside each other and gazed upward at the white ceiling and remembered playing Baby Huey. I was usually Huey, the enormous baby duck in diapers who drooled and puked and pooped and issued guttural gagas to Bea's howling joy. We remembered Mrs. Klinchklonch, the witch woman we invented, who hated children, and how we delighted in describing her monstrous doings. She threw children out the window, dunked them in wells, peppered them vigorously, and drenched them in chocolate sauce. We remembered becoming the Mellolards, a vocal team that appeared when we sat at our little red table in our little red chairs and sang commercials, not real commer-cials, but made-up ones about toothpaste that spurted from the tube and laundry detergent that turned the clothes green and candy that melted in your hand, not in your mouth. We remembered our blue dresses with pinafores and our patent leather shoes that shone with Vaseline and that we held our knees together and folded our hands in our laps and were very, very good. We remembered Mama's embroidered calendar and the tiny wrapped presents that appeared on it every day of December and that our anticipation for Christmas gave us stomachaches, and we remembered baths. We held a washcloth over our eyes so we wouldn't get soap in them and leaned backward, and Mama poured the warm water over our heads with a pitcher, and she heated towels in the dryer and wrapped us in the warm terry cloth, and then Father would lift us, one at a time, high up into his arms and gently lower us into chairs in front of the fire to keep us warm. *Baths were paradise,* said Bea. *They were,* said I, and then she told me she used to pretend to be asleep in the car when we returned late from our grandparents' so that Father would carry her inside, and I told her I knew she was faking and that I had been jealous because I was too big, and I had sometimes worried that he loved her more. I was a crybaby and she wasn't. *You're still a crybaby,* she said. *So true,* I said. *Maybe,* my sister said, *I should have cried more. I always had to be so tough.* We were quiet then.

I'm sorry I was such a wimp, Bea.

Let's go to sleep, she said, and I said, *Yes,* and we did, and I didn't take a pill, and I slept very well.

* * *

How to tell it? asks your sad, crack-brained, crybaby narrator. How to tell it? It gets a bit crowded from here on in—there's simultaneity, one thing happening at Rolling Meadows, another at the Arts Guild, another at the neighboring house, not to speak of my Boris wandering the streets of NYC with my concerned Daisy on his heels; all of this will have to be dealt with. And we all know that simultaneity is a BIG problem for words. They come in sequence, always, only in sequence, so while I sort it out, I will refer to Dr. Johnson. Referring to Dr. Johnson in a pinch is a good bet, our own man of the English language, our wise, fat, gouty, scrofulous, kindhearted, witty glutton, a being of authority, to whom we can all turn in moments of trouble, a cultural *pater familias* who was so important he had his own man document him while he was still ALIVE. And that was the eighteenth century, well before every Tom, Dick, Harry, Lila, and Jane recorded each tawdry, moronic detail of his or her lamentable life on the Internet. (Please note the addition of Lila and Jane; there is no female equivalent of "Tom, Dick, and Harry," which connotes Everyman; Everywoman, alas, is something entirely different.) Grub Street, however, to the great dismay of Dr. Johnson, was churning out countless confessions or faux confessions, just as lurid and hair-raising as today's misery memoirs. But enough. We cite *Rasselas,* a section on marriage, in which our hero offers his appraisal of the sacrament:

Such is the common process of marriage. A youth and a maiden meeting by chance, or brought together by artifice, exchange glances, reciprocate civilities, go home and dream of one another. Having little to divert attention or diversify thought, they find themselves uneasy when they are apart, and therefore conclude that they shall be happy together. They marry, and discover what nothing but voluntary blindness had before concealed; they wear out life in altercations and charge nature with cruelty.

Willful ignorance disguises grim reality: You mean I'm stuck with you? But it's different now, says the savvy reader. That was the old days. We are more enlightened than the Enlightenment, we of the twenty-first century, with our widgets and gadgets and high-speed winklets and no-fault divorce. Ho! Ho! Ho! is my response to you. The sorrows of sex are never-ending. Give me an epoch, and I'll give you a sobbing narrative of conjugal relations turned sour. Can I really blame Boris for his Pause, for his need to seize the day, for snatching the pausal snatch while there was still time, still time for the old-timer he was swiftly becoming? Don't we all deserve to romp and hump and carry on? Dr. Johnson's own sex life remains under wraps, mostly, thank heaven, but we do know that David Garrick told David Hume, who told Boswell, who recorded it in his journal, that after witnessing Dr. Johnson's pleasure one night at the theater, Garrick hoped aloud that the eminent lexi-cographer would return often, but the Great Man averred he would not. "For the white bubbies and the silk stockings of your Actresses," said the Sage, "excite my genitals." We all have ticklers, adaptive or not, and it is our nature to use them. One can be sick with jealousy and loneliness and still understand that.

But there is another aspect of long marriages that is rarely spoken about. What begins as ocular indulgence, the sight of the gleaming beloved, which incites the appetite for around-the-clock rumpty-rumpty, alters over time. The partners age and change and become so accustomed to the presence of the other that vision ceases to be the most important sense. I listened for Boris in the morning if I woke to see his half of the bed empty, listened for the flushing toilet or the sound of him filling the teakettle with water. I would feel the hard bones of his shoulders as I placed my hands on them to greet him silently while he read the paper before going to the lab. I did not peer into his face or examine his body; I merely felt that he was there, just as I smelled him at night in the dark. The odor of his warm body had become part of the room. And when we had our conversations that often went on into the night, it was his sentences I attended to. Alert to the transitions he made from one thought to the next, I concentrated on the content of his speech as it unwound in my mind, and I placed it inside the ongoing dialogue between us, which was sometimes savage, but more often not. It was rare that I studied him. Sometimes after we had done the deed, and he walked naked across the room, I would look at his long pale body with its round belly and his left leg with its blue varicose vein and at his soft well-formed feet, but not always. This is not the voluntary blindness of new attraction; it is the blindness of an intimacy wrought from years of parallel living, both from its bruises and its balms.

During our penultimate call before she was to leave for the month of August, I told Dr. S. what I had never told anyone. A week before Stefan killed himself, the two of us were sitting together on our sofa at home in Brooklyn, waiting for Boris. My brother-in-law had been released from the hospital only two days before. He was taking his lithium, but he had been explaining that it made his mind flat and the world distant. He leaned back on the sofa, closed his eyes, and said, *But even when my head is dead, I love you, Mia,* and I said I loved him, too, and he said, *No, I love you. I've always loved you and it's killing me.*

Stefan was crazy, but he was not always crazy. He wasn't crazy then. And he was beautiful. I had always found him beautiful, worn and disappointed though he was. The brothers resembled each other, but Stefan was much thinner and far more delicate, almost feminine in his features. His manias starved him because he forgot to eat. When he was flying, he went on sex binges with floozies he stumbled over in bars and on book-buying sprees he couldn't afford and, like my friend Nobody, he spouted mysterian philosophies that were sometimes hard to follow. But that day he was in a state of quiescence. I said something about his feeling being a mistake, about all the time we had spent together, that he had come to rely on me, stuttering in confusion, and then my sentences dwindled to silence, but he went on: *I love you because we're the same. We're not like the Commander General.* That was one of Stefan's nicknames for Boris. In belligerent moods, Stefan sometimes saluted his older brother. *Sister Life,* Stefan said, turning his face to me and taking my cheeks in his hands *and he kissed me long and hard and I let him and I loved it and I never should have,* I said to Dr. S. Before Boris walked through the door I had told Stefan that we couldn't and it had been stupid, all the usual claptrap, and he had looked so hurt. And it's killing me. Sister Guilt. His terrible dead face, his terrible dead body.

I knew that I was not to blame for Stefan's death. I knew that he must have decided in a moment of despair that he did not want to ride the dragon anymore, and yet I had never been able to reproduce our conversation aloud, had never been able to get the words out into those open fields under the vast sky. Hearing myself speak, I understood that by declaring our mutual weakness and anger at Big Boris, Stefan had bound himself to me with a kiss. It was not the kiss as such that had mortified me and kept me silent, but what I had felt in Stefan, his jealousy and vengeance, and it was this that had frightened me, not because the feelings belonged to Stefan but because they also belonged to me. The little brother. The wife. The ones who came second.

"But you and Stefan were not the same," Dr. S. said, not long before we hung up.

Not the same. Different.

"In the hospital I felt like Stefan."

"But Mia," Dr. S. said, "you are alive, and you want to live. From what I can tell, your will to live is bursting out all over."

Sister Life.

I listened to myself breathe for a while. I heard Dr. S. breathe through the telephone. Yes, I thought. Bursting out all over. I liked that. I told her I liked it. We are such strange creatures, we human beings. Something had happened. Something unbound in the telling.

"If I were there with you right now," I said, "I would jump into your lap and give you a big squeeze."

"That would be an armful," said Dr. S.

Around the same time, give or take a few days, even weeks, backward or forward, the following events were taking place beyond my immediate phenomenal consciousness, not necessarily in the order presented. They cannot be unscrambled by me or perhaps by anyone, hence in medias res:

My mother is reading *Persuasion* for the third time in preparation for the book club meeting to be held in the Rolling Meadows lounge on August 15. She assumes a position of ultimate comfort for this task. Lying on her bed with three pillows behind her, a soft neck brace to cushion arthritic twinges, hot water bottle for her cold feet, reading glasses for the bridge of her nose to bring the type into focus, and a special-order lap desk that holds the volume in position, she immerses herself in the lives of people she knows well, especially Anne Elliot, whom my mother, Bea, and I all love and chat about as if Kellynch Hall is down the hall, and good, old, long-suffering, sensible Anne might knock on the door at any moment.

Pete and Lola are fighting, a lot.

Daisy, who is still Muriel every evening at the playhouse, becomes Daisy Detective post-performance and trails her sphinx of a father around the city. The man has taken to long nocturnal perambulations, the meaning of which she does not understand. True to her character, Daisy dons flamboyant costumes for her gumshoe expeditions, which (although I know nothing of them or of her life as a spy at the time) seem likely to make her more conspicuous rather than less: Groucho Marx glasses, eyebrows, nose, and mustache; long blond wig with spangly red evening dress; tailored suit and briefcase; bowler hat and cane. Of course, in NYC, where the naked, the nuts, and the outlandish mingle freely with the staid and the conventional, she might have passed hordes of pedestrians without receiving a single glance. At around three in the morning, every morning, Boris returns to the apartment on East Seventieth Street, lets himself in, and vanishes from our daughter's sight, upon which she returns to her apartment in Tribeca, throws herself exhausted onto her bed, and, as she put it to me later, *crashes*.

Simon laughs for the first time. While Lola and Pete lean over the princely crib, their faces contorted with adoration, he looks up at his two devotees, waves all four limbs in a rush of excitement, and chortles.

Abigail works her way through my six slim collections of poems, all faithfully published by the Fever Press in San Francisco, California: *Lost Diction, Little Truths, Hyperbole in Heaven, The Obsidian Woman, Dang It,* and *Winks, Blinks, and Kinks.*

Regina forgets. Neither my mother nor Peg nor Abigail can say exactly when they first notice the decline in their friend's memory. They all forget bits and pieces of recent reality, after all. They, too, occasionally repeat questions or stories, but Regina's forgetting has a different coloring. The three Swans (four when George was alive) have tolerated Regina's vanity, self-absorption, and restlessness (she could not eat at a restaurant without changing tables three times) because she knows how to have fun. She has arranged teas for them and called for tickets to this event and that one. She has told charmingly garbled jokes, and rarely appeared at the door of her friends' apartments without an offering: a flower or decorative box or candleholder picked up somewhere on her life's journey across continents; but the advent of potential thrombosis—"straight to my lungs and I'm dead"— has given her already flighty character an extra propeller that has started to whirl at high speed. Her growing amnesia for appointments, conversations, the location of her keys and purse, her glasses, and some faces (not Swan faces, but others) quickly turns into panic and tears. The deficits the other three joke about as "senioritis" or "old-lady brain" seem to devastate Regina. She has been rushing to her doctor three or four times a week, has sulkily repeated that she simply can't believe, can't *believe* that she, she, Regina, who was once, by marriage anyway, a crucial player in the world of international diplomacy, has ended up in *this place,* a *home—that's what it is, isn't it, a home?* It strikes her as an outrage. And so, little by little, without anyone being able to pinpoint the moment of transformation, the old coquette has alienated herself from her far more stoical friends.

Flora becomes psychological: "Mommy, you know what's funny?"

"No, Flora," says Lola.

"Sometimes I love you so, so, so much, but other times I really, really hate you!"

Ellen Wright calls the other mothers, calmly recounts Alice's story, and arranges a meeting of parents and children at her house. She asks me as well, but I beg off due to Bea and say I will reorient my class toward verses that promote the greater good—mutual understanding, warm camaraderie, melting kindness—although I have no clue how I will achieve this. I do know that the colloquy took place the Sunday after the fatal Friday when Alice poured forth the unsavory details of her persecution. The mothers and daughters (Alice's father is the only male personage in attendance) convene around the time Bea, my mother, and I are having a glass of Sancerre as we prepare our farewell dinner for Bea in my rented kitchen—a succulent roast chicken with garlic, lemon, and olive oil, a new-potato salad, and beans from Lola's garden. The secondhand reports cannot be reassembled perfectly, but the drama unfolds, if not as follows, then in a way very much like it and, as we all know, even eyewitness accounts are hardly reliable, so you will just have to swallow this report as I have decided to render it.

Six tense mothers straggle into the Wrights' living room with sullen, irritable daughters in tow. (Whether or not anyone glances at the large poster of Goya's priest defeating a robber in six frames from the Chicago Art Institute that hangs over the sofa, I cannot say, but it is a great work even in reproduction.) Ellen Wright, who once trained in social work, now employed as an administrator at the Bonden Health Clinic, opens the forum with a short speech, during which she uses the current verb of choice to describe the events in question: *bullying*. She notes its prevalence, its potential damage to *long-term mental health,* notes that girls are sneakier and more underhanded than boys (my adjectives) and that these activities do not go away by themselves; *it takes a village.* I am not responsible for the dead phrases that litter the discourse of pop sociology. Mrs. Wright then articulates a heartfelt desire to listen, to open the floor to all players.

Silence ensues. Several pairs of eyes glare at Alice, who sits between parental buffers.

Mrs.-Lorquat-of-the-frowning-Deity, mother of Jessie, wonders aloud how, when so much of what went on was anonymous, can it be known that her Jessie was even *involved.*

Mrs. Hartley, mother of Emma, pokes her child to prompt words. Several pokes later, Emma, red-faced, confesses to messages cooked up by an ensemble cast. And she names names: Jessie, Ashley, Joan, Nikki, and herself. But they hadn't *really meant it;* it was *just stupid stuff kids do.*

Nikki and Joan alternately make short exclamatory remarks to the effect that they, too, had not intended to do any real harm. It was just that Alice was always talking about Chicago and she was always reading books and acting better than they were and so they thought she was *kinda stuck-up and everything* and so . . .

Mrs. Larsen, mother of Ashley, weary-faced, meek-voiced, inquires innocently of stone-faced daughter: *But I thought you and Alice were such good friends.*

We are!

Peyton, squirming under an avalanche of guilt, shouts the word *liar* and unloads revelations that will come as no surprise to either you or me, while Mrs. Berg tries to dampen her daughter's zeal by saying quietly, *Don't shout, Peyton,* but Peyton shouts anyway that Ashley took the photographs and posted them, that she suggested the Zack deception, and that she, Peyton, went along with it and she *feels bad, really bad.* But Peyton isn't finished. There is more. Peyton says she was scared to tell, *freaked,* because she, Ashley, started a club called the Coven. Before joining the group, each girl agreed to cut herself with a knife and bleed enough to sign her name in blood to a document, in which she swore her allegiance to the other members and promised that their dark alliance would remain a secret *forever.* Peyton produces small scar on thigh of very long left leg as evidence.

This gothic twist on the proceedings, with its air of satanic ritual, creates a stir among the adults. Poor Mr. Wright, a chemistry professor, accustomed to shepherding premed students through the peaks and valleys of predicting formulas with polyatomic ions, is uncomfortable in the extreme and begins an intense examination of his fingernails. Mrs. Lorquat issues a gasp, as bloody documents are even more offensive to God than D. H. Lawrence. The mothers of Nikki and Joan, friends for life, seated side by side, drop their jaws in unison. Aghast questioning of Coven members ensues.

Ashley commences crying.

Alice watches.

Ellen watches Alice.

What Alice thinks at this juncture we do not know, but it is more than likely that she feels some satisfaction that the pubescent witches of Bonden have been exposed. At the same time, Alice isn't going anywhere. She is staying in town with the little she-devils, her friends.

Commentary: *The instruments of darkness tell us truths*. What are they? Boys will be boys: rambunctious, wild, kicking, hanging from the trees. But girls will be girls? Gentle, nurturing, sweet, passive, conniving, stealthy, mean?

We all start out the same in our mothers' wombs. We, all of us, when floating in the amniotic sea of our earliest oblivion, have gonads. If the Y chromosome didn't swoop in to act on the gonads of some of us and make testes, we would all become women. In biology, the Genesis story is reversed: Adam becomes Adam out of Eve, not the other way around. Men are the metaphorical ribs of women, not women of men. Most of the time, it's XX = ovaries, XY = testes. The renowned Greek physician Galen believed that female genitalia were the inversion of the male's and vice versa, a view that held for centuries: "Turn outward the woman's, turn inward, so to speak, and fold double the man's and you will find the same in both in every respect." Of course, outward trumped inward every time. Inward was definitely worse. Exactly why, I can't say. Outward is pretty vulnerable, if you ask me. In fact, castration anxiety makes a lot of sense. If I were carrying my reproductive organs on the outside, I'd be pretty damned nervous about that delicate little package, too. As with the human navel, the ancient sex model had innies and outies, which meant that an innie might just surprise you by becoming an outie, especially if you went around behaving like someone who already had an outie. That hidden, folded-over yard might just make a sudden appearance. Montaigne, great literary peak of the sixteenth century that he was, subscribed to the innie/outie thesis: "Males and females are cast in the same mold, and, education and usage excepted, the difference is not great." He repeats a well-known story about Marie-Germain, who was just plain Marie until the age of twenty-two in Montaigne's version (fifteen in other versions), but one day, due to strenuous exercise (jumping over a ditch while chasing pigs), the male rod popped out of her, and Germain was born. Incredible, you say. Impossible, you say. But there is a particular family in Puerto Rico and another in Texas with a genetic condition in which XY looks for all the world exactly like XX. In other words, phenotype disguises genotype, until puberty that is, when late in the game the little girls become little boys and grow up to be men. Carla turns into Carlos! Darling daughter becomes darling son without a surgical instrument in sight. What is certain is that *in utero,* the sex differentiation story is fragile. Things can and do get all mixed up.

Mia, you are saying, get to the point. Relax, breathe deeply, and I will make my rhetorical turn shortly. This is a question of sameness and difference, of what Socrates in the *Republic* calls a "word controversy." He tells his interlocutor, Glaucon, that they find themselves in "eristic wrangling" because they hadn't bothered to inquire "what was the sense of 'different nature' and what was the sense of 'same nature' and what we were aiming at in our definition when we allotted to a different nature different practices and to the same nature the same." The Great Father of Western Philosophy is working out the man/woman problem for his utopia and comes to rest (uneasily, I think, but he rests nevertheless) on this: "But if the only difference is that the female bears and the male begets, we shall not admit that it is a difference relevant for our purpose." The purpose: whether women should be given the same education as men and then allowed to rule beside them in the Republic.

Mostly the same, but different in parts, mostly in those lower begetting and bearing parts? Or different in *kind*? Thomas Laqueur, bless his heart, has written a whole book on the subject. Once the innie-outie theory collapsed, sometime in the eighteenth century, women were no longer inverted men; we were wholly OTHER: our bones, nerves, muscles, organs, tissues, all different, another machinery altogether, and this biological alien was ever so delicate. "While it is true that the mind is common to all human beings," wrote

Paul-Victor de Sèze in 1786, "the active employment thereof is not conducive to all. For women, in fact, this activity can be quite harmful. Because of their natural weakness, greater brain activity in women would exhaust all the other organs and thus disrupt their proper functioning. Above all, however, it would be the generative organs which would be the most fatigued and endangered through the over exertion of the female brain." The thought-shrivels-your-ovaries theory had a long and robust life. Dr. George Beard, author of *American Nervousness,* argued that unlike the "squaw in her wigwam," who focused on her nether regions and popped out one child after another, the modern woman was being deformed by thinking, and to prove it, he cited the work of a distinguished colleague who had measured highly educated uteruses and found them to be only half the size of those never exposed to learning. In 1873, Dr. Edward Clarke, following the noble Beard, published a book with a friendly title: *Sex in Education: A Fair Chance for Girls,* in which he argued that menstruating girls should be banned from the classroom and cited hard evidence from clinical studies conducted at HARVARD on intellectual women which had determined that too much knowledge had made these poor creatures sterile, anemic, hysterical, and even mad. Maybe that was my problem. I read too much, and my brain exploded. In 1906, the anatomist Robert Bennett Bean claimed that the corpus callosum—the neural fibers that bind the two halves of the brain together—were bigger in men than in women and hypothesized that the "exceptional size of the corpus callosum may mean exceptional intellectual activity." Big thoughts = Big CC.

But no one utters such nonsense now, you say. Science has changed. It is based on facts. And yet, colleagues of my wayward husband are hard at work measuring brain volume and thickness, scanning its oxygenated blood flow, injecting hormones into mice, rats, and monkeys, and knocking out genes left and right to prove beyond all doubt that the difference between the sexes is profound, predetermined by evolution, and more or less fixed. We have male and female brains, different not only for reproductive functions but in countless other *essential* ways. While it is true that the mind is common to all human beings, each sex has its own KIND of MIND. Dr. Renato Sabbatini, for example, distinguished neurophysiologist, who was a postdoc fellow at the MAX PLANCK INSTITUTE, enumerates a long list of differences between us and them and then announces: "This may account, scientists say, for the fact that there are many more [male] mathematicians, airplane pilots, bush guides, mechanical engineers, architects and race car drivers than female ones." Study all you want, girls, you will never solve a Riccati equation. Why? The wigwam idea returns without bringing in Native Americans (it is no longer possible to demonize or idealize the wigwam; we must retreat to peoples who can no longer be insulted): "Cave men hunted. Cave women gathered food near the home and took care of the children." But not to worry, our esteemed professor assures us (citing an even higher paternal AUTHORITY, that great " 'Father' of sociobiology" at HARVARD, Edward O. Wilson), you might not have evolved to make it as a bush guide, but "human females tend to be higher than males in empathy, verbal skills, social skills and security seeking, among other things, while men tend to be higher in independence, dominance, spatial and mathematical skills, rank-related aggression, and other characteristics." Our superior "verbal skills," if we follow the professor's own logic, explain why women have dominated the literary arts for so long, nary a man in sight. I am sure you have also noticed that when the titans of contemporary literature are referred to, both in academia and in the popular press, the numbers of women among them are, quite simply, overwhelming.

I am happy to say that my own (or used-to-be own) Boris would not agree with Dr. Sabbatini. Up to his ears in rats as my old man is and attached to evolution and genes as he also is, he knows that genes are expressed through the environment, that the brain is plastic and dynamic; it develops and changes over time in relation to what's *out there*. He also knows, despite our commonalities, that people are not rats and that the higher executive functions in human beings can be decisive in determining what we become, and he knows that good science one day can become bad science the next, as was true of the sensational discovery in 1982 that the corpus callosum, the selfsame fibrous brain-hemisphere connector of Dr. Bean, especially one part of it known as the splenium, is actually LARGER in women than in men. This study, soon to be trumpeted to the masses by *Newsweek* magazine, claimed not that women were intellectually superior (an idea never advanced in the annals of human history) but, rather, that we of the large CCs have greater communication between the hemispheres of our brains, which in *Newsweek* was conveniently translated as "women's intuition." But then a study of Korean men and women found that the pesky thing was bigger in men. Koreans must be special. Then another study found no difference. Other studies followed: a little bigger, a little smaller, about the same, no difference. In 1997, Bishop and Walsten, the authors of a review of forty-nine studies on the corpus callosum, concluded: "The widespread belief that women have a larger splenium than men and consequently think differently is untenable." Whoops. But the myth is still circulating. One simpleton, eagerly spewing his own brand of pseudoscience, has dubbed the CC the "caring membrane of the brain."

It is not that there is no difference between men and women; it is how much difference that difference makes, and how we choose to frame it. Every era has had its science of difference and sameness, its biology, its ideology, and its ideological biology, which brings us, at last, back to the naughty girls, their escapades, and the instruments of darkness.

We have several contemporary instruments of darkness to choose from, all reductive, all easy. Shall we explain it through the very special, although dubious otherness of the female brain or through genes evolved from those "cave women gathering food near the home" thousands of years ago or through the dangerous hormonal surges of puberty or through nefarious social learning that channels aggressive, angry impulses in girls underground? Surely our Ashley, contrary to the good doctor's analysis, is deeply interested in "social dominance" and "rank-related aggression," despite her XX status, just as my old friend Julia was, when I was a sixth grader in an earlier era and I opened a piece of paper that had been left on my desk and read the words, formed by letters cut out of a magazine, "Everybody hates you because you are a big fake." And I recall wondering, Am I a fake? Hadn't I checked out from the library books with tiny print that were too hard for me? Did that prove they were right? The note stirred the psychic muck within me—guilt and weakness and a worry that as much as I wanted to be admired and loved, I wasn't worthy—and I, wimp and crybaby, allowed them to taint me. Fake! I wasn't fake enough. Glory to artifice, to the clown mask, to the Dracula face to hide the softness. Put on your armor and pick up your lance. Hail a bit of falseness if it protects you from the vipers.

Truisms are often untrue, but that cruelty is a fact of human life is not one of them. We must go closer, so close that we smell the blood from their cuts and the frisson of secrecy and theatrical danger the girls found in the Coven. We must be so close that we feel the pleasure they took in hurting Alice and so close to Alice that we can see how in her vulnerability and her need to be so very, very good, she defanged herself, just as I had before her.

But, I told myself, you are no longer twelve. Your fangs may not be the sharpest, but they have grown back and now you can act. I made seven phone calls and explained to seven mothers that I wanted to take a week off, but that during that week each of the girls had to write her story of what happened in either poetry or prose. Two pages minimum. The rest of the class would be spent dealing with that material in one way or another. I was forceful. Although I heard some murmurs of concern about "going over all that again," no one opposed me in the end, not even Mrs. Lorquat, who seemed genuinely shaken by the whole ungodly mess.

Dear Mom,

Dad has moved into a hotel. I'm not sure what's going on exactly, but we're going to have dinner on Thursday, and he has promised to talk to me, to be totally honest. I told him that he really should write to you, and he said he would, but I have to tell you he sounds awfully sad on the telephone, all slowed down. He's no open book, Mom, but I will keep you posted. A week and a

half and I'll be in Bonden, my little Mammy
dear, and will pop through your door and fling
my arms around you!

Love from your own Daisy girl

A. Boris dumped the Pause.
B. The Pause dumped Boris.
C. The affair was still on, but the duo had
   decided the pausal quarters were too small,
   hence hotel.
D. The two parted by mutual agreement.
E. None of the above.

A was preferable to B, B to C. D was preferable to B.
E was an unknown quantity, or X. Much inward
churning and burning over A, B, C, D, and X. Considerable spinning of satisfying fantasies of prodigal
spouse prostrate or kneeling in state of keen remorse.
Other, less satisfying fantasies of spousal heart broken
by Frenchwoman. Some introspective activity on the
conflicted state of own worn and tattered heart. No
crying.

And then, on Wednesday evening, around nine-thirty,
while I was reading Thomas Traherne aloud to myself
in a very low voice as I lay on the sofa, my face covered

in a mud mask of a green hue, a concoction I had purchased because its makers promised it would soften and purify an older face like mine (they did not state this explicitly, but the euphemism "fine lines" on the label had made their intention clear), I heard him next door, the volatile Pete, howling two well-known expletives, an adjective for the sex act and a noun for female genitalia, over and over again, and with every verbal assault my body stiffened as if from a blow, and I walked to the glass doors that opened to the yard and stood looking out toward my neighbor's low modest house, but the windows revealed no persons. It wasn't entirely dark yet, and the sky's deep blue was streaked with darker trails of graying clouds. I opened the doors and stepped onto the grass and into the hot summer air, and I heard Simon wail, then the front door slam. I saw a racing shadow that was Pete, heard the car door slam, the ignition, the revving motor, and the skid of tires as the Toyota Corolla vanished down the empty street and took a violent left, presumably into town. Then, framed in the window, I saw Lola walk into the living room with Simon, her head bent over him, bouncing the child in her arms as Flora trailed after them like a sleepwalker. They were all whole.

I didn't move for a few minutes. I stood there with my bare feet in the warm grass and felt immeasurably sad. All at once, I felt sad for the whole lot of us human beings, as if I had suddenly been transported skyward and, like some omniscient narrator in a nineteenth-century novel, were looking down on the spectacle of flawed humanity and wishing things could be different, not wholly different, but different enough to spare some of us a little pain here and there. This was a modest wish, surely, not some utopian fantasy, but the wish of a sane narrator who shakes her red head with its slices of gray and mourns deeply, mourns because it is right to mourn the endless repetitions of meanness and violence and pettiness and hurt. And so I mourned until the door opened, and my three neighbors emerged from the house and came across the lawn, and I took them in.

There were four, really, because Flora had brought Moki. As she walked toward me over the grass dressed only in her Cinderella underpants, she spoke urgently to him, telling him it was okay, that he mustn't worry, mustn't cry, that it would be all right. The child patted the air beside her and kissed it once and when we were inside, she ran to the sofa, curled up in the fetal position, and squeezed her eyes tightly shut. I noticed she was not wearing her wig. I sat down beside Flora, beckoned to Lola by pointing at a chair, and watched her lower herself into it as if she were an old woman with sore joints, her face oddly expressionless. She did not appear to have shed any tears—her cheeks were dry and the whites of her eyes were untouched by redness—but her chest rose and fell as she breathed deeply, like a person who had been running. I placed my hand gently on Flora's back. She opened her visible eye, took me in, and said, "You're green."

My hand flew to my face as I remembered the beauty

product, rushed off to remove it, returned to the room, and noticed that more than anything Lola looked exhausted. She was wearing a thin paisley bathrobe of some synthetic material that had fallen open at the neck so that it exposed much of her right breast. Her blond hair hung in disordered clumps over her eyes, but she made no effort to adjust the robe or push away the hair. She was limp, beyond effort. Simon whimpered as he pressed the crown of his head against his mother's arm, but she didn't move. I took the baby from her and began to pace, jiggling him as I walked back and forth across the floor. Without turning to look at me, she said in a voice hard with determination, "I will not go back there tonight. I do not want to be there when he comes home. Not tonight." I offered them my bed, to which she said, "We can sleep there, all four. It's a king, right?"

We did sleep there, all four or five of us, depending on how you counted. After giving Lola a couple of shots of whiskey from the Burdas' stash of hard liquor, I rocked Simon to sleep and laid him on the bed, a fat ball of babyhood in blue pajamas with feet, who breathed loudly from his chest, tiny lips pursing and unpursing automatically. I dug out a small blanket I had hidden away and wrapped him up in it to protect him from the air-conditioning and then carried in the unconscious Flora, who snorted once when I pulled the blanket over her, but she quickly rolled over and settled into deep sleep. After I returned, Lola and I sat together for a while. She did not want to talk about

Pete. I asked her about the row, but she said that their fights were stupid, that they were always about nothing, nothing that was important, that she was tired, tired of Pete, tired of herself, sometimes even tired of the children. I said very little. I knew that for the time being I was the open air, the place to put the words, not a real interlocutor. And then, without a transition of any kind, she began to tell me that for three years after she had started school as a child, she had not uttered a word. "I talked at home, to my parents, to my brothers, but I never said anything in school, not to anybody. I don't remember much about preschool, but I remember a little about kindergarten. I remember Mrs. Frodermeyer leaning over me. Her face was really big and close. And she asked me why I didn't answer her. She said it wasn't polite. I knew that. I wanted to tell her that she didn't understand. I just couldn't." Lola looked at her hands. "My mom says that sometime in the first grade I started whispering in school. She was overjoyed. Her kid had whispered. And then, little by little, I guess I just got louder."

After Lola was nestled beside her children on the bed, I sat down on the edge and stroked her head for about twenty minutes. She's only two years older than Daisy, I said to myself. I thought of her, Lola, the silent little girl who couldn't talk in school. The anxiety of speaking in a place that isn't home, that's outside, that's strange. It had a name, as so many things do, selective mutism, not so uncommon in young children. I thought then of a young woman who had been a patient with me in the hospital, and I tried to remember her name, but I couldn't. She hadn't spoken either, not a word. Thin and white and blond, she had made me think of a tubercular revenant from the Romantic age. I saw her as she wandered stiffly up and down the hallway, hunched over, long pale hair drawn over her face like a veil, carrying a plastic pitcher she held very close to her mouth so she could spit into it, sometimes silently, sometimes noisily hawking up gobs of mucus from her lungs, which made the other patients snicker. Once, I had seen her dart behind a sofa in the common area, crouch down, disappear from sight, and then, after a moment, I heard the hoarse roar of her vomiting into the pitcher. Inside out. Keep the outside out. Seal me shut, tight as a drum. Close my eyes. Shut my mouth. Bar the doors. Pull down the shades. Leave me be in my wordless sanctum, my fortress of madness. Poor girl, where was she now?

I found a spot beside Flora and eventually fell asleep, despite the slumberland concert provided by my overnight guests: the whistling of congested little Simon, the masticatory noises of Flora as she sucked and chomped on her index finger, and the restless murmurs and single word emitted by Lola. Several times, in a small high voice, she said, "No." Although I remained in bed with them, my mind roamed as was its wont onto thoughts of Boris and Sidney and the Pause and the sex diary in hiatus. I thought of writing about the innumerable dreams from which I had woken in full riotous orgasm or perhaps about F.G., whom I had called the Grazer because he was a nibbler and a chewer, who moved up and down my body as if it were a delectable green field. I then allowed myself several minutes of extreme irritation over the biogenetic fantasy that it was possible to calculate accurately the percentage of gene influence as opposed to environmental influence on human beings and began writing a scathing critique in my head, but the last thing I remember, which softened my mood considerably, was the RETURN TO TRAHERNE and his poem "Shadows in the Water," which I had read several times to myself only hours earlier. It was prompted, I believe, by an idle musing about Moki and whether he lay invisible among us, the strong, wild little boy with long hair who flew only slowly, but needed comfort after the paternal eruption, needed pats and kisses from his very short, plump, newly wigless authoress.

> O ye that stand upon the brink,
> Whom I so near me through the chink
> With wonder see: what faces there,
> Whose feet, whose bodies do ye wear?
>> I my companions see
>> In you, another me.
> They seemed others, but are we;
> Our second selves these shadows be.

I woke to Pete, not in the flesh, but to his voice on the phone. It was not an angry voice but a composed one, polite but strained, asking for "my wife." I couldn't see the visitors—the bed was empty—but I heard them in the kitchen. Flora was singing nonsense; there was the clink of dishes and the dull bang of some object hitting another, which was then followed by the unmistakable smell of toast.

Lola took the call in the bedroom while I held Simon and supervised the second course of Flora's breakfast, toast with jam, which she waved in the air between bites as she marched back and forth across the black and white tiles, still singing. The babe barfed milk all over my pajama top. The mild odor of the regurgitated milk, the stain that seeped through the cloth and wet my skin, the squirming, bucking body I held securely to my chest brought back the old days with my own Daisy girl, my fierce, agitated infant Daisy. I had walked the floors with her for hours in the first months of her life as I breathed soothing words into her tiny curl of an ear, repeating her musical name over and over until I felt her tense chest and limbs relax against me. I had had only one child, and it hadn't been easy. And Lola had two. And Mama had had two. When Lola emerged from the bedroom, she paused in the door and smiled an enigmatic smile. I wondered whether Pete-of-the-Blasting-Expletives had begged forgiveness and caused that smile or whether I looked ridiculous holding the now howling Simon. Before she gathered her two charges, one in each arm, and trudged heavily across the lawn back to her sick, sorry, and sober husband, the laconic Lola said, "It never changes. It's always the same. You'd think I'd wise up, wouldn't you? It gave him a start, though, when I wasn't home, scared him. Thanks, Mia."

Good old Mama Mia, who lies alone in the great king bed with its wide-open spaces, a blank expanse of white sheets she fills up with inner speech and memory, a whirligig of words and thoughts and aches and pains. Mia, Mother of Daisy. Mia, Mother of Loss. Once, Wife of Boris. *But O the heavy change, now thou art gone.* O Milton on the brain. O Muse. O Mia, rhapsodic boob, blustering bimbo, pine no more! Roll up your troubles, wipe up your stains, kick off your shoes, and sing something silly for your own sake as you sail on kingless in that great groaning schooner of a bed, not a tawdry queen for you, Bard of the Laughing Countenance, but a king.

Thursday afternoon, Boris wrote the following. *Explication de texte* included:

Mia,

It has ended with [*proper name of French love object*]. I am staying in the Roosevelt. In the last two weeks I have thought more about my life than at any other time. It has been a black period for me. I even called Bob [*psychiatrist friend doing research at Rockefeller. The even here is an example of the radical understatement of which B.I. is capable. He has always stubbornly, vehemently resisted any and all kinds of psychotherapeutic intervention. Calling Bob suggests desperation.*] It has become obvious to me that I have acted precipitously in order to escape parts of myself, parts of my past, and you have suffered because of this. [*Read: mother, father, Stefan, and remember, Boris is a scientist. His prose is going to thud forward. It seems to go with the job.*] When [*proper name of young Francophone bewitcher*] and I were together, I found myself talking to her a lot about you. This, as you probably can imagine, did not go over well. She was also annoyed by my domestic habits or lack of them. [Read: *cigar butts piling up in ashtrays, recently read papers from* Nature, Science, Brain, Genomics, *and* Genetics Weekly *stacked in piles on every surface of apartment, clothes thrown on floor. Also read: Despite three postdocs, claims he is unable to master the technology of dishwasher, clothes washer, or dryer.*] I came to see her as someone I had idealized from afar, and I suspect that she had done the same with me. [*The unreal no longer occludes the real.*] Working together and living together are different. [*You bet they are, Bub.*]

I would like to see you, Mia, and talk to you. I
have missed you. I am sharing a meal with
Daisy tonight.

Boris

I concluded that reality had to coincide with either
A or B or D. Both C and X appeared to have been
eliminated.

If this little epistle strikes you as inadequately emotional
in light of what had happened, I cannot disagree, but
then you haven't lived with the man for thirty years.
Boris is scrupulously honest. I knew every word he
had written was both considered and truthful, but I
also knew that the man was prone to a wooden
demeanor. In some people, this indicates a genuine
lack of feeling underneath, but this is not true of Boris.
The entire letter turns on three sentences: "It has been
a black period for me." "I even called Bob," and "I
have missed you."

Boris, I replied. I have missed you, too. Your letter is
oblique, however, as to who left whom? You can
understand that from my point of view, this matters.
If the Pause threw you onto the street, and this act
caused a reconsideration of our marriage, it is very
different from an alternative, which is that you decided

to leave her, after reconsidering your relationship with her because of your former relationship with me. Those two are also distinct from a mutual decision to part ways. Mia

(If he wasn't going to write "Love," I sure as hell wasn't going to stoop to that devilishly tricky noun.)

Excitement usually comes at a clip. Agitation in one corner is often mirrored by a similar hubbub in another. There is no rhyme or reason to this. Correlation is not cause. It is just "the music of chance," as one prominent American novelist has phrased it. Long, lazy, uneventful periods are followed by sudden bursts of action, and so it was that the very morning after Pete's screeching exit from his wife and children, another equally dramatic departure was taking place over at Rolling Meadows, which I discovered when I paid my daily visit to my mother. Regina had gone to the beauty parlor to have her long hair "professionally put up," packed two suitcases, called the three Swans to announce that she couldn't bear her incarceration in the Home any longer, and then, after slamming the door to her apartment, had made a speedy march down the hall (or as speedily as was possible for Regina with her delicate leg). My mother and Peg (Abigail was indisposed) had followed the fugitive to the front door, where they cross-examined her about what in heaven's name she was up to. Her three daughters had counseled her to stay. She had ended it with Nigel, hadn't she, after the story about the gold watch and the buxom barmaid? Within seconds, they concluded that Regina had no idea where she was going. Her flight was pure flight, that is to say, flight without a destination. Moreover, she had rambled on about Dr. Westerberg, whom she claimed had threatened her, and said that if she didn't "get away" she was convinced he would "put her away." After a quarter of an hour, my mother and Peg had cajoled Regina back to her apartment. A tearful scene had followed, but in the end, she had seemed resigned to her fate and had promised her friends to stay put.

Chapter 2: Only a couple of hours before I arrived, my mother had knocked on Regina's door to check on her state of mind. Regina had refused to let her in. Not only that, she had claimed she had pushed the furniture up against the door as a barricade against enemies, especially Westerberg. When my mother reported this, she shook her head sadly. I could only sympathize. When paranoia arrives, it does little good to tell the paranoiac that the fear is unfounded. I understood. My brain had cracked, too. And so, after trying to reason with her unreasonable friend, my mother had gone to the nurse to report on the developments in No. 2706, and the medical staff had been summoned, including the diabolical Westerberg, and the door had been unlocked, and the furniture had been removed from the doorway, and after that Regina herself had been removed to a hospital in Minneapolis for "testing."

When she finished this story, my mother appeared

to gaze straight through me. She looked sad. Sadness was chasing us all, it seemed. I was sitting beside her and took her hand but said nothing.

"I don't think she will come back," my mother said. "She won't come back here, anyway."

I squeezed my mother's thin fingers and she squeezed mine in return. Through the window I saw a robin alight on the bench in the courtyard.

"She had spunk," my mother said. I noted her use of the past tense.

Another robin. A pair.

My mother began to talk about Harry. All losses led back to Harry. She had often spoken of him, but this time she said, "I wonder what would have happened to me if Harry hadn't died. I wonder how I would have been different." She told me what I already knew, that after her brother's death, she had decided to be perfect for her parents, never to give them any grief, ever again, that she had tried so hard, but it had not worked. And then she said what she had never said before, in a barely audible voice: "Sometimes I wondered if they wished it had been me."

"Mama," I said sharply.

She paid no attention and continued talking. She still dreamed of Harry, she said, and they weren't always good dreams. She would find his body lying somewhere in the apartment behind a bookshelf or chair, and she couldn't understand why he wasn't in his grave in Boston. Once in a dream, her father had appeared and demanded to know what she had done with Harry. When Bea and I were children, she said, she had had periods of terror that something would take us from her, an illness or accident. "I wanted to protect you from every kind of hurt. I still do, but it doesn't work, does it?"

"No," I said. "It doesn't."

My mother's melancholy didn't last, however. I told her Boris had been in touch, which both cheered and worried her, and we weighed several possible outcomes and discussed what I wanted from my husband, and I discovered I didn't exactly know, and we went over Daisy's acting life and how precarious it all was, but how damned good the kid was, after all, and then Bea called while I was still there, and I listened to my mother laugh at some witticism of my sister's, and over dinner she laughed again, hard, at one of my own. She embraced me tightly when we parted, and I sensed that her earlier gloom had been dispelled, not forever, of course, but for the evening. Twelve-year-old Harry would always be there, the ghost of Mama's childhood, the empty figure of her parents' hopes and of her guilt for having lived. I imagined my six-year-old mother as I had seen her in an old photograph. She has red hair. Although it is impossible to see the color in black and white, I add the redness in my mind. Little Laura stands beside Harry, a head shorter than he is. They are both wearing white sailor suits with navy trim. Neither child is smiling, but it is my mother's face that interests me. By chance, she is the one looking ahead, into the future.

* * *

Below, without commentary, an epistolary dialogue made possible by racing twenty-first-century technology that took place the following day between B.I. and M.F. on the scenarios A, B, or D, and so on.

B.I.: Mia, does it really matter what happened? Isn't it enough that it is over between us, and I want to see you?

M.F.: If the story were reversed, and I were you, and you I, wouldn't it matter to you? It is a question of the state of your heart, old friend of mine. Heart dented by rejection *à la française,* unhappy and surprisingly helpless alone, Husband decides it may be better to begin reconciliation proceedings with Old Faithful; or, Seeing the error of his ways, Spouse penetrates his Folly (ha, ha, ha) and has revelation: Worn Old Wife looks better from Uptown.

B.I.: Can we dispense with the bitter irony?

M.F.: How on earth do you think I would have made it through this without it? I would have stayed mad.

B.I.: She broke it off. But the thing was already broken.

M.F.: I was broken, and you came to the hospital once.

B.I.: They wouldn't let me come. I tried to come, but they refused me.

M.F.: What do you want from me now?

B.I.: Hope.

I couldn't answer "hope" until the next day. The reversal I had dreamed of had come, and I felt as hard as a piece of flint. My answer to the big B. arrived in the morning: "Woo me."

And he, in high Romantic style, wrote back, "Okay."

Mr. Nobody had not written in some time, and I began to worry. We had been lobbing balls back and forth on the subject of play, that is, playing with play. He threw me a Derridian fastball first, the endless play of logos, round and round we go without end and without resolution, and it's all in the text, the doing and the undoing, then I threw back Freud's "Remembering, Repeating, and Working Through," in which the esteemed doctor tells us that transference, the spooky place between analyst and patient, is like a *spielplatz,* a playground, a terrain somewhere between illness and real life, where one can become the other, and then he hurled back a beautiful quote from the great mountain himself: "If anyone tells me that it is degrading to the Muses to use them only as a plaything and a pastime, he does not know, as I do, the value of pleasure, play, and pastime. I would almost say that any other aim is ridiculous." I fired back with Winnicott and Vygotsky, the latter dead since 1934 but a brand-new love of mine, and after that, my spouting phantom went silent.

I decided too much time had passed: "Everything okay? I'm thinking of you. Mia."

The book club is big. It has been sprouting up like proverbial fungi all over the place, and it is a cultural form dominated almost entirely by women. In fact, reading fiction is often regarded as a womanly pursuit these days. Lots of women read fiction. Most men don't. Women read fiction written by women and by men. Most men don't. If a man opens a novel, he likes to have a masculine name on the cover; it's reassuring somehow. You never know what might happen to that external genitalia if you immerse yourself in imaginary doings concocted by someone with the goods on the inside. Moreover, men like to boast about their neglect of fiction: "I don't read fiction, but my wife does." The contemporary literary imagination, it seems, emanates a distinctly feminine perfume. Recall Sabbatini: we women have the gift of gab. But truth be told, we have been enthusiastic consumers of the novel since its birth in the late seventeenth century and, at that time, novel reading gave off an aroma of the clandestine. The delicate feminine mind, as you will remember from past rants inside this selfsame book, could be easily dented by exposure to literature, the novel especially, with its stories of passion and betrayal, with its mad monks and libertines, its heaving bosoms and Mr. B.'s, its ravagers and ravagees. As a pastime for young ladies, reading novels was flushed pink for the risqué. The logic: Reading is a private pursuit, one that often takes place behind closed doors. A young lady might retreat with a book, might even take it into her boudoir, and there, reclining on her silken sheets, imbibing the thrills and chills manufactured by writerly quills, one of her hands, one not absolutely needed to grip the little volume, might wander. The fear, in short, was one-handed reading.

On Saturday at five in the afternoon, the Rolling Meadows Book Club met in the library over small sandwiches and even smaller glasses of wine to discuss the novelist Jane Austen, author of *Persuasion,* ironic observer, precise dissector of human feeling, stylist from heaven, and an author who did away with perverted monks but retained her own version of virtue rewarded. Both loved and detested, she has kept her critics hopping. "Any library is a good library that does not contain a volume by Jane Austen," said America's literary darling Mark Twain. "Even if it contains no other book." Carlyle called her books "dismal trash." But today, too, she is accused of "narrowness" and "claustrophobia" and dismissed as a writer for women. Life in the provinces, unworthy of remark? Women's travails, of no import? It's okay when it's Flaubert, of course. Pity the idiots.

You may recall that I had been asked to introduce the proceedings. With some editing here and there and taming of my prose from the incendiary to the palatable, as well as additional rigmarole about the Great Jane teetering between two literary eras and inventing a new road for the novel, the above paragraph gives you an idea of what I said, so we won't bother to rehearse it here.

The DISCUSSANTS: The three remaining Swans, my mother, armed with well-marked copy of book in question; Abigail, looking more doubled over than ever and exceedingly frail, dressed in elaborately embroidered blouse depicting dragons; and the mild, good-natured Peg, with her bright side showing, as well as three ladies new to me: Betty Petersen, with a sharp chin and sharper gaze, had made extra money for the family as the author of humorous texts for a greeting card company; Rosemary Snesrud, former eighth-grade English teacher, and Dorothy Glad, widow of Pastor Glad, who had once presided at the small Moravian Church on Apple Street.

The SETTING: two sofas upholstered in an alarming green-and-violet print of aggressive foliage facing each other, two stuffed chairs, far less excited in appearance, also parked across from each other, all of which circled long oval coffee table with one unstable leg, which caused it to lurch every now and again when especially perturbed. Three windows on far wall with view of courtyard and gazebo. Bookshelves with volumes, most of which were lying wearily on their sides or leaning with a desultory air against a divider, but too few of these to qualify for the noun *library*. General hush in building interrupted only by squeaking walkers in nearby hallway and the occasional cough.

The CONTROVERSY: Should the young Anne Elliot have been persuaded by her vain, silly, profligate father, her vain and cold sister, Elizabeth, and her well-meaning, kind, but very possibly misguided older friend, Lady Russell, to break with Captain Wentworth, with whom she was madly in love because he had only prospects, no fortune? As you may have noticed, in general members of book clubs regard the characters inside books exactly the way they regard the characters outside books. The facts that the former are made of the alphabet and the latter of muscle, tissue, and bone are of little relevance. You may think I would disapprove of this, I, who had endured the ongoing trials of literary theory, who had taken the linguistic turn, witnessed the death of the author and somehow survived *fin de l'homme,* who had lived the life hermeneutical, peered into aporias, puzzled over *différance,* and worried about *sein* as opposed to *Sein,* not to speak of that convoluted Frenchman's little *a* versus his big one, and a host of additional intellectual knots and wrinkles I have had to untie and smooth out in the course of my life, but you would be wrong. A book is a collaboration between the one who reads and what is read and, at its best, that coming together is a love story like any other. Back to the controversy at hand:

Peg looks on the bright side. Because Anne gets Wentworth in the end, all is well.

Abigail strongly disagrees: "Wasted years! Who has time to waste years?" Adamant statement followed by table limping to one side. Glass slides. Grabbed by Rosemary Snesrud. Does not fall.

Uncomfortable silence pertaining to waste, my own silence among the other silences, a wondering silence about wasted years, about the not done, the not written.

Dorothy Glad injects extraliterary not-at-all-glad possibility: "He might have drowned at sea! Then she would never have found love."

I suggest sticking to the text itself, as it was written without that particular shipwreck.

My mother holds up imaginary scale and weighs familial duty against passion. Imagine the pain of alienating one's family. That has to be considered, too. There was no easy solution for Anne. For the motherless Anne, breaking with Lady Russell was tantamount to breaking with her mother.

Rosemary S. defends *my* mother. According to the Snesrud philosophy, life's decisions are "sticky."

Betty Petersen brings in unsavory Elliot cousin destined to inherit family baronetcy: "She might have hitched herself to that snake in the grass, if her friend, what's-her-name, hadn't given her the dope on him. Lady Russell was completely snowed."

Abigail, irritation mounting, insists that stepping on one's desires is deforming. She makes strong pronouncement accompanied by feeble bang on the table's surface: "It mutilates the soul!" Table nods in agreement, but Peg clicks her tongue. Talk of mutilation threatens brightness of all kinds.

My mother gazes soberly at her friend Abigail, understanding that it is not Anne's soul that has been mutilated. The crooked Abigail is trembling. I notice how skeletal her arms are under her dragon blouse. I suffer irrational worry that the strength of her emotion will shake her fragile bones to the breaking point, and I deflect the conversation to men and women and the question of constancy, one close to my heart. What do the discussants think of Anne's argument about women and men in her conversation with Captain Harville?

"Yes, we certainly do not forget you so soon as you forget us. It is, perhaps, our fate rather than our merit. We live at home, quiet, confined, and our feelings prey upon us. You are forced on exertion. You have always a profession, pursuits, business of some sort or other, to take you back into the world immediately and continual occupation and change soon weaken impressions."

With the exception of myself, there wasn't a woman in the room under seventy-five. The two schoolteachers, three housewives, and part-time greeting card wit may all have been born in the Land of Opportunity, but that opportunity had been heavily dependent on the character of their private parts. I remembered my mother's words: "I always thought I'd go on and get at least a master's degree, but there was so little time and not enough money." A sudden image of my mother at the kitchen table with her French grammar book came back to me, her lips moving as she silently repeated the verb conjugations to herself.

Harville brings out the BIG GUNS to refute Anne, albeit in a highly civil manner.

> ". . . I do not think I ever opened a book in my life which had not something to say upon woman's inconstancy. Song and proverbs, all talk of woman's fickleness. But perhaps you will say, these were all written by men."
>
> "Perhaps I shall.—Yes, yes, if you please, no reference to examples in books. Men have had every advantage of us in telling their own story. Education has been theirs in so much higher a degree; the pen has been in their hands. I will not allow books to prove anything."

Of course, the pen that inscribed those words was in Austen's hand, and a neat hand it was, too. The woman's handwriting had all the clarity and precision of her prose. And the pen, as it were, Dear Reader, is now in my hand, and I am claiming the advantage, taking it for myself, for you will notice that the written word hides the body of the one who writes. For all you know, I might be a MAN in disguise. Unlikely, you say, with all this feminist prattle flying out here and there and everywhere, but can you be sure? Daisy had a feminist professor at Sarah Lawrence, most decidedly a man, married, too, with children and a Yorkie, and on the rampage for women, a noble defender of the second sex. Mia might really be Morton for all you know. I, your own personal narrator, might be wearing a pseudonymous mask.

But back to our story: Not surprisingly, the women of Rolling Meadows are in Anne's corner. Even our Peg of Permanent Sunshine allows that there were times at home with her five "wonderful children" when she longed for some diversion, when *her* feelings preyed upon *her,* and then, in a moment of startling revelation, the resident optimist confesses that there had been days when she had been "pretty darned tired and blue," and that in her experience far more men have the gift for forgetting women than women have for forgetting men. Weren't they the ones who turned around and got married just months after their wives "passed away"? (I suppressed comment that Boris hadn't even waited for me to die.)

Betty offers humorous quote: "I am woman. I am invincible. I am pooped!"

Laughter.

Rosemary notes the exception to the rule of women waiting, pining, hoping: Regina.

Titters.

My mother rises to fellow Swan's defense: "She had fun, though!"

Abigail nods, regards my mother lovingly, and says

in a loud, if hoarse voice, "Who's to say we shouldn't all have had more fun!"

Who is to say? Not I surely. Not my mother, not Dorothy, not Betty, not Rosemary, not even Peg, although the latter proffers the buoyant comment that they are having fun, well, aren't they, right now, at this "very minute"? And the *carpe diem* sentiment does, in fact, brighten the entire room, if not literally, then figuratively.

After that, there was some pleased nodding, some silent sipping, and some tangents onto the movie being shown in the screening room at seven, *It Happened One Night,* followed by some mooning over Clark Gable and chatter about how films used to be so much better and, good grief, what had happened? I volunteered that Hollywood films were now made exclusively for fourteen-year-old boys, an audience of limited sophistication, which had drained the movies of even the hope of sprightly dialogue. Farts, vomit, and semen had taken its place.

I seated myself beside Abigail then and held her hand for a little while. She asked me to come see her. The request was not casual. She had some urgent business to discuss, and it had to happen in the next couple of days. I promised, and Abigail began the protracted rigors of pulling her walker toward her, getting herself into a standing position, and then moving, one small, careful step after another, toward her apartment.

Within minutes, the book club was over. And it had ended before I could say that there is no human subject outside the purview of literature. No immersion in the history of philosophy is needed for me to insist that there are NO RULES in art, and there is no ground under the feet of the Nitwits and Buffoons who think that there are rules and laws and forbidden territories, and no reason for a hierarchy that declares "broad" superior to "narrow" or "masculine" more desirable than "feminine." Except by prejudice there is no sentiment in the arts banned from expression and no story that cannot be told. The enchantment is in the feeling and in the telling, and that is all.

Daisy sent this:

Hi, Mom. Dinner with Dad was okay. He seems a little better. He was shaved at least. I think he's really, really embarrassed. He said he hoped that you would be able to see his "interlude" for what it was. He also mentioned "temporary insanity." I said that's what you had, and he said, maybe he had it, too. Mom, I think he's sincere. It's been awful for me to have you two against each other, you know. Love and kisses, Daisy

And yet, I could not leap at Daisy's father. As I meditated on our story, I understood that there were multiple perspectives from which it could be viewed. Adultery is both ordinary and forgivable, as is the rage of the betrayed spouse. We are not unworldly, are we? I had endured my own French farce, starring my fickle, inconstant husband. Was it not time "to forgive and forget," to use that inveterate cliche?" Forgiveness is one thing, forgetfulness another. I could not induce amnesia. What would it mean to live with Boris and the memory of the Pause or Interlude? Would it now be different between us? Would anything change? Can people change? Did I want it to be the same as it had been? Could it be the same? I would never forget the hospital. BRAIN SHARDS. For better or for worse, I had become so entwined with Boris that his departure had ruptured me, sent me screaming into the asylum. And wasn't the fear I had felt old, the fear of rejection, of disapproval, of being unlovable, a fear that may be older even than my explicit memory? For months, I had drowned in anger and grief, but over the summer my mind had unconsciously, incrementally begun to change. Dr. S. had seen it. (How I missed her, by the way.) Reading Daisy's letter, I felt those subliminal, not yet articulated thoughts rise upward, form sentences, and lodge themselves securely somewhere between my temples: *Some part of me had been getting used to the idea that Boris was gone forever.* No one could have been more shocked than I by this revelation.

And now the curtain must rise on the following Monday, when seven uncomfortable girls and a poet, laboring to hide her own anxiety, sat around a table at the Arts Guild. A torpor seemed to have taken hold of all seven young bodies, as if an invisible but potent gas had been unleashed in the room and was swiftly putting them all to sleep. Peyton had folded her arms on the table and laid her head down. Joan and Nikki, seated side by side as always, sat in heavy silence, eye-lined lids cast downward. Jessie, elbows propped on the table surface, rested her chin in her hands, a vacuous expression on her face. Emma, Ashley, and Alice all appeared limp with exhaustion.

I looked at each of them for a moment and, on a sudden impulse, burst out singing. I sang them Brahms's lullaby in German: *"Guten Abend, gute Nacht, mit Rosen bedacht . . ."* I don't have a sweet voice but my ear is good, and I let the vibrato go so it sounded suitably absurd. The look of surprise and confusion on their faces made me laugh. They did not laugh with me, but at least they had been rattled out of their fatigue. It was time for my speech, and I made it. The gist of it was that a single story with seven characters can also be seven stories, depending on the identity of the narrator. Every character will regard the same events in her own way and will have somewhat different motives for her actions. Our task was to make sense of a true story. I had given it a title: "The Coven." This was met with a round of wordless murmurs. We would meet every day this week to make up for the lost classes. Today each girl would read her text and we would talk about it, but in the following four days, we would trade places and write the story from the point of view of someone else. Jessie would become Emma, for example, and Joan, Alice, and Jessie, Ashley, and I, Nikki, and so on. Eyes widened, worried looks exchanged across the table. By the end of the week, we would have a story authored by the entire class. The trick was, we would have to agree, more or less, on the content.

To be honest, I had no idea whether this would work. It was not without its risks. Note: The now famous psychology experiment at Stanford in 1971. A group of young men, all college students, took on the roles of either prisoners or guards. Within hours the guards began tormenting their prisoners and the experiment was stopped. The theater of cruelty made real? Performance becomes the person? How malleable were the seven?

I began with a short summary of my experience: my suspicions during class, my bafflement about the Kleenex, and my dim awareness that some plot was cooking. I also mentioned my involvement in a similar story as a girl. I did not say which role I had played. You, friend out there, will mostly be spared the tedium of early adolescent prose; it is worse than the poetry. (Not one child chose to describe the hex scandal in verse.) Suffice it to say that the clumsy and often ungrammatical narrations were not harmonious. After every reading, the refrains "I never said that!" "It was your idea, not mine!" "That's not how it was at all!" rang out loudly. Some of the tiffs were of no importance, when and where and who. "You put the dead cricket in the formula, not me!" "Ask my mom. She saw you coming out of the bathroom with blood running down your arm, remember?" Nevertheless, there were recurring justifications for the plot: They had all liked Alice at first, but then, as time went on, she had distinguished herself in ways they didn't like. She had been Mr. Abbot's "pet" in history class and was always raising her hand with the answer. She bought her clothes in Minneapolis in a *department* store, not at the Bonden mall. She read all the time, which was "boring." Ashley's synopsis included the fact that Alice had been given a starring role in the school play, and after this "lucky break," she had metamorphosed into "a big snob." What had begun as a "little fun" among the conspiratorial witches to "get back at Alice" had somehow, mysteriously, run wild, of its own accord. There were no agents in this version of the story, just currents of feeling, very much like spells, that had pulled the girls hither and yon. Bea and I used to have a phrase when we were growing up that described such actions well: "accidentally on purpose." When I mentioned this, there were sheepish smiles all around, except of course from Alice, who was hard at work scrutinizing the table's surface.

She read last. Despite the ugliness of the tale she had to tell, the girl had cast herself as its heroine in the mode of Jane Eyre or David Copperfield, those wronged orphans I had loved so much when I was her age, and she had worked hard on the story. Heavily adjectival and hyperbolic though it was, and not free of diction errors ("torturous" for "tortured"), it articulated both her intense need to be inside the group and the agony of being an outcast. Listening to her, I guessed that although her dramatis persona would not endear her to all the members of the Coven, finding it had been a boon for her. The victim came out well in her version of events, if only because Alice had dressed up her alter ego in gothic conventions that had been conveniently aided by the memorable storm that had cracked the heavens as I lay in bed that night in June. Apparently, while "hanging out" at Jessie's house, the girls had jointly decided not to look at or answer Alice when she spoke, to behave as if she were both invisible and inaudible. After half an hour of this treatment, our heroine had escaped into the "pelting rain, weeping violently, her hair whipping in the wind" while "lightning flashed crooked in the sky." When she arrived home, this tragic creature was "soaked to the skin and frozen to her bones with crazily chattering teeth." Although Alice may not have enjoyed the Coven's version of Meidung, she had certainly taken pleasure in writing about it. Alice the literary character served a redemptive function for just plain Alice, who was going into the seventh grade. Her narrative ended with the words "Never before have I felt such deep, unbearable despair."

I did not smile. I remembered.

Poor Peyton, whose remorse was already in full bloom, cried and blew her nose.

Jessie did not look at Alice, but she apologized in a mortified whisper.

Nikki and Joan wriggled with unease.

Ashley and Emma remained implacable.

I sent them off with their assignments. I gave Ashley and Alice to each other, paired Peyton and Joan, Nikki and Emma, and because seven is uneven, I took Jessie for myself, and she was given the task of writing as the mostly ignorant poetry teacher.

Boris wooed.

Mia,

I was just a fat-headed guy full of pain.

Boris

(Reference: T. R. Devlin, played by Cary Grant, to Alicia Huberman, played by Ingrid Bergman, near the end of *Notorious*. The hero is, if I remember correctly, carrying his drugged-by-poison beloved down the stairs when he makes this remark. Boris and I had seen the film at least seven times together, and every time B.I. had become tearful over this succinct explanation for Mr. Devlin's genuinely wretched treatment of the divine Miss Huberman. I was not unmoved by this bit of wooing. No, I won't hedge: I was moved. It would never do to replace Cary with Boris or me with Ingrid. When I imagine my slightly rotund in the middle, bespectacled neuroscientist puffing and groaning as he bears frizzy-headed fifty-five-year-old versifier down enormous Hollywood staircase, the illusion is lost. But that is not the point. We must all allow ourselves the fantasy of projection from time to time, a chance to clothe ourselves in the imaginary gowns and tails of what has never been and never will be. This gives some polish to our tarnished lives, and sometimes we may choose one dream over another, and in the choosing find some respite from ordinary sadness. After all, we, none of us, can ever untangle the knot of fictions that make up that wobbly thing we call a self.)

From Bea, after having been informed of the Boris/ Mia developments:

Just remember, Baby Huey, we all screw up.
Love, B.

From Nobody, finally:

Kidney stones.

Poor Mr. Nobody, my high-flying partner in dialogue, had been brought down by those excruciating pebbles. I wished him a swift recovery.

* * *

I had learned to wait for some time after knocking for Abigail to appear at the door. My visits had been fairly regular. I had gone either alone or with my mother, and we had both worried about our mutual friend since her fall. She seemed to dwindle daily, and yet, the force of her personality remained strong. In fact, what attracted me to Abigail was her rigidity. This is not usually regarded as a desirable feature in human beings, but in her it seemed to have developed as resistance to a particular midwestern ethos of frightened conformity. Abigail had sewn and embroidered and appliquéd in quiet but adamant insurrection. I now knew the story of Private Gardener. She had married him on an impulse just before he headed off for the Pacific, but when he returned after the war, he brought the war back with him. Plagued by nightmares, fits of rage, and bouts of ferocious drinking to the point of unconsciousness, the man who had come home bore little resemblance to the boy she had vowed to "love, honor, and obey," but then, as she put it, "I didn't really know him from a hole in the wall to begin with." One day, to her immense relief, her spouse went AWOL. A year later, she received a letter of contrition from the ex-soldier asking her to join him in Milwaukee. Because the very thought of it turned her "cold as an ice cube," Abigail refused, asked for a divorce, and the grade school art teacher was born.

Her mother had taught her to embroider, but it wasn't until after her marital debacle that she had joined the sewing group, understood that "she needed to do it," and her double life began. Over the years she had created many works, both conventional and subversive or, as she put it, "the real ones" and the "fakes." She sold the fakes. One by one, she had been showing me the real ones, and the strangeness of Abigail's project had become more and more apparent. Not all of them were spiteful or sexual in nature. There was an embroidery of delicate mosquitoes in various sizes, replete with traces of blood; a joyous image of a figure straight out of *Gray's Anatomy,* organs exposed but dancing; another of a gargantuan woman taking a bite out of the moon; a large and oddly poignant tablecloth that featured women's underclothing: a corset, bloomers, a chemise, stockings, panty hose, a thick brassiere of the old style, a girdle with garter belt, and a baby doll nightgown; and there was a remarkable portrait sewn into a pillow in tiny crosshatch stitches she had done years before of herself in a chair weeping. The tears were sequins.

When she opened the door, my friend looked tiny. The tremor had gone to her head, and her chin wobbled as she stood in front of me. She was beautifully attired in narrow black pants and a black blouse covered with red roses. Her short sparse hair was combed behind her ears, and through the lenses of her narrow glasses her eyes were as intensely focused as I had ever seen them.

That afternoon, Abigail and I made arrangements.

She reclined on her sofa and spoke to me about her death. She had no one but a niece, a dear woman, but she would never understand the amusements. "She'll get my money, what there is of it." She then quoted a line from my first book of poems: *We were mad for miracles and ships with lace*. "That's us, Mia," she said. "We're two peas in a pod." I was flattered even though I was forced to see us round and green in the pod on a kitchen counter. Then she abruptly shifted metaphors, from the organic to the mechanical: "I'm an alarm clock, Mia, ready to go off, and when I do, there'll be no going back. I hear myself ticking." She had made it all legal in her will, she said. I was to have the secret amusements and do with them whatever I wanted. The papers were in the top drawer of her small desk. I should know. The key could be found in the little Limoges egg box, and I was to take it out now and open her drawer; there was something she had to show me, a photograph slipped inside a manila envelope right on the top.

Two young women wearing tuxedos are standing with their arms over each other's shoulders, grinning, one dark, whom I guessed had to be Abigail, and one blond. The blonde has a cigarette in her right hand. They look giddy and jaunty and careless and enviable.

Abigail lifted her head. Then she nodded. She nodded for several seconds before she spoke. "She had the same name as your mother. Her name was Laura. I loved her. We were in New York. It was nineteen thirty-eight."

Abigail smiled. "Hard to believe that whippersnap-per is me, huh?"

"No," I said, "it's not hard at all."

When I embraced her before I left, I felt her bones under the rose-covered shirt, and they felt no larger than chicken bones, my Abigail, who couldn't sit up straight anymore, who had the shakes and had once loved a girl named Laura in New York City in 1938, a remarkable woman, an art teacher for children and an artist, an artist who knew her Bible. The last thing she said to me was: "He shall come down like rain upon the mown grass: as showers that water the earth." Psalm 72:6.

Being the other is the dance of the imagination. We are nothing without it. Shout it! Shimmy, kick your heels, and leap. That was my pedagogy, my philoso-phy, my credo, my slogan, and the girls were trying. I can say that for them. Their "I"s had been scrambled, and they worked to find the meaning that comes with another role, another body, another family, another place. Their success varied, but that was to be expected.

Jessie as Mia wrote, "I had some kind of feeling about the girls' problems, but they didn't tell me. I remembered going into seventh grade and the messy stuff that happened to me, but it was a long, long, long time ago . . ." (Fair enough.)

Peyton as Joan wrote, "I've been Nikki's best friend

since first grade and I basically do what she does. When I saw she wasn't afraid to cut herself, I decided to do it, too, even though I felt pretty yucky about it."

Joan as Peyton: "I want to be a cool girl, but I'm immature. I like sports better, and I went along with doing bad things to Alice on account of I wanted to be cool."

Nikki as Emma: "I suck up to Ashley because I think she can make me feel better about myself and it's fun to be around her because she doesn't really care about getting into trouble. When she decided to make me swallow that part of the dead mouse's tail, I did it, even though it was disgusting. I'm like her slave. She dares people and I like falling for the dares. My little sister has muscular dystrophy and it worries me a lot so being with my friends and doing stupid things helps me not think about it."

Emma as Nikki wrote, "I like showing off and acting wild, dressing up in black clothes, putting on crazy makeup that makes my mom upset. Being mean to Alice was a way to show off."

Ashley wrote, "I'm Alice, Miss Perfect. I like Chicago because it's a big city with lots of stores and museums and my mom escorted me to those artsy, fartsy places and now we can't go anymore. I used to be Ashley's friend, but I think I'm too sophisticated for her. I'm an only child and my parents spoil me, buying me expensive clothes and sending me to ballet in St. Paul. I use words the other kids don't know just to make them feel stupid. I'm so moral I don't know how to have any fun, and I look all hurt and weepy whenever somebody says the tiniest little thing. If I hadn't been such a wimp, the girls wouldn't have been able to do anything to me."

Alice wrote: "I hate Alice because she was Charlene in the play. It made me putrid with jealousy. She didn't comprehend my deceit, and that made it smooth for me, as smooth as jelly from the jar. I could feign to like her, but injure her violently behind her back. My brothers and sisters are always kicking and hitting each other, slamming doors, and my house is a huge mess, and I have to take meds for a mood disorder, and my mom is always yelling at me for not taking them . . ."

Recriminations, disavowals, and gasps punctuated the entire hour, but the fact that Ashley had assigned her own disorder, whatever it was, to Alice was by far the most disquieting revelation. Neither Alice nor Ashley had been able to penetrate each other's psyches or find any mutual sympathy, but when Alice, unknowingly or knowingly, let go of Ashley's secret, all the girls were quiet until Peyton yelled, "But Ashley, you said Alice had a mood disorder, not you." The trick of trading first-person subjects had doubled back on itself. Ashley, it seemed, had already been playing the game.

1) I will check the refrigerator for juice and milk and remember to buy them if we are low.

2) I will promise to read *Middlemarch* all the way
   through. (That goes for *The Golden Bowl*, too.)
3) I will not interrupt you when you are writing.
4) I will talk to you more.
5) I will learn to cook something besides eggs.
6) I will love you.

Boris

   I read the list several times. To be frank, I did not
believe the first five. That would require a revolution
of the sort I had ceased to believe in. My world turned
on number six, because, you see, Boris had loved me.
He had loved me for a long time and the question was
not so much whether he meant it—I believed he meant
it—but whether there was self-delusion at work. Could
he really leave his explosive Interlude behind him or
would her phantom be in residence with us for the
rest of our days? But worse, if Boris had lurched out
the door once, what would prevent him from doing it
again? When I replied, that was exactly what I asked
him.

Regina returned to Rolling Meadows, but not to the
independent-living quarters. She was placed in a
special unit on the other side of the grounds for
Alzheimer's patients, even though she hadn't been
diagnosed with the disease. After "the incident," the

powers that be (mostly benevolent, but by no means infinitely tolerant) had made the decision that she could not be trusted. She had to be watched. My mother and I found her sitting in a small bare room—nearly identical to my own hospital room at Payne Whitney but with no view of the East River—on a grim cot with a blue cover, her beautiful long white hair disheveled and hanging around her face. When my mother walked through the door, Regina cried out, "Laura!" and stretched her arms out for her friend. The two hugged each other and then, still in the embrace, rocked back and forth for a minute or so. When they separated, Regina looked at me as if she were searching, and I realized that the fallen Swan had forgotten my name, possibly my entire being, but my mother rescued her comrade by identifying me as soon as she understood that I was missing from Regina's mental storehouse.

The two women talked, but Regina talked more. She chattered about her ordeal—the tests, the kind doctor and the nasty one, the endless questions about presidents and the time of year and could she feel this pinprick and on and on. She broke down and blubbered but recovered quickly and within seconds began to wax nostalgic. Hadn't it been wonderful on the other side, in Independent? She had her apartment there with all her "lovely things," and they had been only a short walk away from each other, and oh my dear, the spider plant, had anyone watered it? And now look at her, in exile with "the crazies" and the people who "drooled and peed and dirtied their pants." If only she could get back to the other side. I saw my mother open her mouth and then close it. If Regina wanted to remember the "home" she had detested as a paradise, who was she to destroy the illusion? As we were leaving, the old woman lifted her head, tossed back her messy locks, and beamed. She blew kisses to us and sang out in a high brittle voice, "Come back, Laura. Won't you? I've missed you terribly. You will remember to come back."

Just before I closed the door, I took a last glance at Regina. She looked deflated, as if the theatrical good-bye had taken all the air out of her.

Outside in the hallway, my mother stopped. She pressed both hands to her chest, closed her eyes, and said under her breath, "It's so bitter."

"What, Mama?"

"Old age."

The Lola, Pete, Flora, and Simon soap opera had been one of repetition without much difference, as Lola herself had acknowledged, but now circumstances conspired to make some difference, and the difference was money. As much as I liked my Chrysler Buildings and had indulged Lola by listening to her business plans, I hadn't been optimistic. The poor young woman had had little time to devote to her jewelry and, all in all, the prospects for success had seemed poor. And then, out of the blue, just as it happens in novels, especially eighteenth- and nineteenth-century novels, Lola's godmother, a single, frugal lady who had worked as a bursar at St. Joseph's College for fifty years, died, and this elderly deus ex machina left her goddaughter a complete set of Wedgwood china and a hundred thousand dollars. (Let us be fair: This happens all the time in twentieth- and twenty-first-century LIFE; it just happens less often in twentieth- and twenty-first-century NOVELS.)

And so, at least for a while, Lola was flush, and more important, the money was hers, not Pete's. In the same week, a small store in Minneapolis agreed to sell Lola's creations. They were partial to the architectural earrings, especially the Leaning Towers of Pisa. Joy was abroad at the neighbors'. We celebrated Friday night after a hard week with the witches. (I will report on that later. Chronology is sometimes overrated as a narrative device.) My mother, Peg, Lola, and the two poppets were in attendance. I invited Abigail, but she was too weak, she said, to make the journey, even though we offered to drive her the few yards to the Burdas'.

Lola wore pink. My mother wore Simon most of the evening, and the two had a high time. The little man was singing. When my mother sang to him, he sang back, admittedly in tones that were unconventional, possibly even bizarre, but he sang nevertheless, and his flutelike emissions were the source of much hilarity. Flora ran wild and wigless and whispered to Moki and stuffed cake into her mouth. I was careful to fawn and crow over her so she would not feel that her infant brother won every cuteness battle. Peg shone brightly. At a family gathering, she was in her element, and her presence added sugar to what was already a sweet occasion.

I asked Lola if Pete was traveling, but no, her husband had stayed home. He had felt uncomfortable, she said, as the only man, and he had urged her to go alone and have fun. While Peg and my mother occupied her children, Lola and I stepped into the bedroom where we had all spent the night in the king, and she told me that having the money made her feel different. "I didn't do anything to earn it," she said, "but now that it's mine, I feel more important, somehow, freer, and Pete's happier. It's like he can breathe a little and not worry so much. And then there's the Artisans' Barn, and suddenly they like my stuff, so he doesn't think my jewelry is just useless tinkering."

We stood together and looked out the window. I had become attached to the view and to the summer sky, especially when the sun fell and colored it in blues and lavenders and pinks, and I could watch the cloud formations above the field and the copse of trees and barn and silo that grew black and flat as the evening progressed. A study in repetition. A study in mutability. And Lola said she would miss me when I went home, and I said I would miss her. She wondered what I was going to do about Boris, and I told her about the wooing, and she smiled. From the other room, I heard the women laugh and Flora squeal and, after a few seconds, the noise of Simon crying.

Lola and I stayed put, however, for another few seconds, just looking out the window in silence before she made her way back to the party to comfort her baby boy.

Homo homini lupus. Man is a wolf to man. I found the sentence in a work by that grand old pessimist Sigmund Freud, but it apparently comes from Plautus. Sad but true. Look around you. Look even at the little girls, at their grasping for status and admiration, at their ruthless tactics, at their aggressive joys. As their "I"s continued to revolve from one child to the other during the week, I sometimes lost track of which person was playing whom, but they had no such problems with identification. Although there were few further revelations, the story I had entitled "The Coven" began to take shape. Ashley had been toppled. She fell with her lie. I doubt whether she would have felt any genuine remorse had she not been caught, but she suffered her loss of power keenly. She was a survivor, however, and began to adjust to her new role in the group: On Wednesday she made a formal apology to her victim, and this, whether sincere or not, helped lift her reputation among the others.

Emma had been jogged hard by the mention of her ill sister, but the sympathy the girls felt for her lot as the healthy but ignored sibling softened her considerably, and she volunteered amendments to the story and her role in it that I thought were brave: "It made me happy when Alice cried." Jessie's narcissistic platitudes had taken a beating. She understood that she had believed in herself too much. She'd fallen for the wicked plot with hardly a thought. As the week went on, Peyton cried less and less and relished her roles as the other girls more and more. The catharsis of theater. In fact, by Thursday it was obvious that a tacit script had already been written, and the children had thrown themselves into their own melodrama with gusto. Alice lost something of her stature as romantic heroine, but her suffering was acknowledged by all, and she entered the lives of her tormentors with such zeal that by Friday, Nikki cried out, "Oh my God, Alice, you like being the mean one!" Joan, of course, agreed.

The story they all took home on Friday was not true; it was a version they could all live with, very much like national histories that blur and hide and distort the movements of people and events in order to preserve an idea. The girls did not want to hate themselves and, although self-hatred is not at all uncommon, the consensus they reached about what had happened among them was considerably softer than the one advanced by the Viennese doctor I quoted earlier. As for me, by the end, I felt my encounter with the Coven had done me good. I was hugged by all seven, my praises were sung, and I was presented with a gift: a violet box filled with an odiferous soap, hand lotion in a bottle of an undulating shape, and a container of large crystals for the bath tied up in a lilac bow. What more could anyone ask for?

And then my Daisy blew into town. This tired expression, with its Wild West connotations, nevertheless suits the beloved offspring. The girl has a windy quality, an ability to stir things up without really doing much. When she jumped out of the cab, large leather bag over her shoulder, its zipper gaping open to reveal messy contents, attired in tiny T-shirt, man's vest, cut-off jeans, boots, a straw fedora, and enormous sunglasses, she seemed to embody agitation, excitement—in short: a small tornado. She's a beauty, too. How Boris and I produced her is a puzzle, but the genetic dice fall every which way. Neither of us is homely, and my mother, as you know, believes me still to be beautiful, but Daisy is the real thing, and it's hard not to look at the child when she's around.

She's an affectionate little devil, too, always has been, a hugger and a kisser and a nose rubber and a stroker, and when we got our arms around each other on the doorstep, we hugged, kissed, nose-rubbed, and stroked for a couple of minutes before we let go. And, as it sometimes happens, it wasn't until that moment that I understood how much I had missed her, how I had pined for my daughter, but I did not, you will be happy to know, burst into tears. There may have been a touch of wetness in the vicinity of my ducts, but nothing more.

We spent the evening at my mother's and, although I remember only bits of what we said, I do remember the animation in my mother's face as she listened to Daisy tell us stories about the theater and Muriel and her nights trailing her father and how he hadn't discovered his "tail" until she confronted him outside the Roosevelt with the words "What the hell is going on, Dad?" And I recall that my mother had more news of Regina. She had been rescued by one of her daughters. Letty had arrived and was making arrangements to move her mother to Cincinnati, where there was a "home" very close to Letty and her family. My mother confessed to not knowing how that would all go, but it was certainly preferable to the "horrible jail cell" in the Alzheimer's unit.

The very next day, we were told that Abigail had had a massive stroke. She was alive, but the woman we had known had vanished. She did not know where she was or who she was. The alarm clock had gone off. The very old languish and die. We know that, but the very old know it far better than the rest of us.

They live in a world of continual loss and this, as my mother had said, is bitter.

I saw her for a few minutes over in Care two days later. My mother did not want to come. I understood why; the specter of losing every faculty that made life life was too close to her. Abigail was lying on her side; her curved spine meant that her head was near her knees, so she occupied only a small part of the bed. Her eyes flickered open every now and again, but their irises and pupils were empty of all thoughts, and when she breathed she rasped loudly. My friend's thin gray hair looked a little greasy and uncombed, and she was wearing a flowered hospital gown she would have detested. I smoothed her hair back. I talked to her, told her I remembered everything, would get the will from the drawer when it was time and would do everything in the world to get the secret amusements into a gallery somewhere. And before I left, I leaned over and sang into her ear very softly, the way I used to sing to Daisy, a lullaby, not Brahms, another one. A nurse startled me when she came through the door behind me, and I lurched back, embarrassed, but she was cheerful, matter-of-fact, and said it would be fine to stay, though somehow then I couldn't. Two days later, Abigail was dead and I was glad.

* * *

I wrote to Nobody about her, about her works and the long-ago love affair. I don't know why I told him. Maybe I wanted an answer of some grandeur. I got it.

Some of us are fated to live in a box from which there is only temporary release. We of the damned-up spirits, of the thwarted feelings, of the blocked hearts, and the pent-up thoughts, we who long to blast out, flood forth in a torrent of rage or joy or even madness, but there is nowhere for us to go, nowhere in the world because no one will have us as we are, and there is nothing to do except to embrace the secret pleasures of our sublimations, the arc of a sentence, the kiss of a rhyme, the image that forms on paper or canvas, the inner cantata, the cloistered embroidery, the dark and dreaming needlepoint from hell or heaven or purgatory or none of those three, but there must be some sound and fury from us, some clashing cymbals in the void. Who would deny us the mere pantomime of frenzy? We, the actors who pace back and forth on a stage no one watches, our guts heaving and our fists flying? Your friend was one of us, the never anointed, the unchosen, misshapen by life, by sex, cursed by fate but still industrious under the covers where only the happy few venture, sewing apace for years, sewing her heartbreak

and her spite and spleen and why not? Why?
Why not? Why? Why not?

In all his bleakness, he made me feel better, strangely
better. Why? Although for the first time I wondered
if Mr. Nobody couldn't just as well be Mrs. Nobody.
Who knew? I wasn't so sure he was Leonard anymore.
But I realized I didn't care. He or she was my voice
from Neverland, from neverness, from Why, not
Where, and I liked it that way.

If I ever do anything really stupid again, nail
me to the wall.

Your Boris

Daisy was standing behind me when I read this
message on the screen, and I felt her hands on my
shoulders. "What're you going to say, Mom? Tell me,
Mom."

"I'll have my staple gun ready."

"Oh, Mom," she groaned. "He's trying, can't you
see? He feels bad."

My daughter rolled back the desk chair I was sitting
in, jumped into my lap, and began cajoling and whee-
dling me to say something encouraging back to dear
old Pa. She pulled at my earlobes and pinched my nose
and used various accents—Korean, Irish, Russian, and

French—to plead with me. She leapt off my lap and soft-shoed and shuffle-ball-changed and waved her arms and wished loudly for the reunion of the aging couple, one Mommy and one Daddy, Sun and Moon or Moon and Sun, the double orbs in her childhood sky.

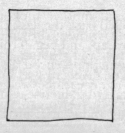

On the day of Abigail's funeral, it rained, and I thought it was right that it should rain. The rain came down on the mown grass, and I remembered the words she had stitched in needlepoint: O *remember that my life is wind*. Rolling Meadows was heavily represented in the pews that afternoon, which meant there were a lot of women, since women were the ones who lived there, mostly, anyway, although the lecherous Busley showed up on his Mobility Scooter, which he parked in the aisle, toward the back. I saw the niece, who looked old, but then she was probably in her seventies. My mother had been asked to speak. She clasped her speech tightly in her lap, and I sensed she was nervous. She had tried on several black outfits before we left, worrying about collars and pressing and what may or may not have been a spot on a skirt, and she finally decided on a tailored cotton jacket and pants with a blue blouse that Abigail had always admired. The minister, a man with little hair and a suitably grave demeanor, could not have known our mutual friend very well because he uttered falsehoods that made my mother stiffen beside me: "A loyal member of our congregation with a generous and gentle spirit."

My small, elegant mother took the steps to the pulpit carefully but without difficulty, and once she had adjusted her feet and reading glasses, she leaned toward her listeners. "Abigail was many things," she said, her voice quavering, hoarse, emphatic. "But she was not a generous and gentle spirit. She was funny, outspoken, smart, and if the truth be told, angry and irritable a lot of the time." I heard a couple of women laugh behind me. My mother went on and with each sentence I could feel her warming to her subject. They had met in the book club the day Abigail shocked her fellow members by denouncing a novel they were reading that had won the PULITZER Prize as "a complete load of stinking crap," a verdict my mother had not opposed but would have worded differently, and she went on to praise Abigail's creative ability and the many works of art she had produced over the years. She called what Abigail had made art, and she called Abigail an artist, and Daisy and I were proud to have such a grandmother and such a mother. I knew Mama wouldn't weep for Abigail. I don't think she wept for Father. She was a true stoic; if there's nothing to be done about it, away with it. The Swans were dying, one by one. We are all dying one by one. We all smell of mortality, and we can't wash it off. There is nothing we can do about it except perhaps burst into song.

We must leave us for a while, leave me and Daisy and the bright Peg, too, sitting beside Daisy, leave my mother as she stands there giving testimony to her friend. We are going to leave her even though she shone that day and later she was congratulated heartily by many for telling what was generally agreed to be something true because it is well known that the dead often go to their graves wrapped up in lies. But we are going to leave us there at a funeral as it rains hard beyond the stained glass windows, and we'll let it unfold just as it did then, but without mention.

Time confounds us, doesn't it? The physicists know how to play with it, but the rest of us must make due with a speeding present that becomes an uncertain past and, however jumbled that past may be in our heads, we are always moving inexorably toward an end. In our minds, however, while we are still alive and our brains can still make connections, we may leap from childhood to middle age and back again and loot from any time we choose, a savory tidbit here and a sour one there. It can never return as it was, only as a later incarnation. What once was the future is now the past, but the past comes back as a present memory, is here and now in the time of writing. Again, I am writing myself elsewhere. Nothing prevents that from happening, does it?

Bea and I have been skating on the rink over by Lincoln school, and we are waiting for our father to pick us up, and we see him coming in the green station wagon. On the way home, he whistles "The Erie Canal," and Bea and I smile at each other in the back seat. At home, Mama is lying on the bed reading a book in French. We jump on the bed, and she feels our feet. They are so cold. *Ice,* she says the word *ice*. Then she strips off our four socks and takes our naked skating feet and puts them under her sweater on the warm skin of her stomach. Paradise Found.

Stefan is sitting on the sofa, gesticulating as he makes his points. As I look at him, I worry. He is too alive. His thoughts are pressing ahead too quickly, and yet I am ignorant then of what will happen. I am innocent of the future, and that state, that cloud of unknowing, is impossible for me to retrieve.

Dr. F. tells me to push. Push now! And I push with all my might and later I discover I have broken blood vessels all over my face, but what do I know about it then, nothing, and I push, and I feel her head, and then voices cry out that her head is coming out of me, and it does, and there is the sudden slide of her body from mine, me/she, two in one, and between my open legs I see a red, slimy foreigner, with a little bit of black hair, my daughter. I remember nothing of the umbilical cord, do I? Nothing of the cutting. Boris is there, and he is weeping. I don't shed a tear. He does. Now I remember! I said that he had never bawled in real life, but that's wrong. I had forgotten! He is standing there right now in my mind crying after his daughter is born.

I am walking into the AIM gallery, a women's cooperative in Brooklyn, to attend the opening of a show called The Secret Amusements.

I am standing beside Boris in our apartment on Tompkins Place. *Do you promise to love him, comfort him, honor and keep him in sickness and in health; and forsaking all others, keep thee only unto him, as long as ye both shall live?*

Well, do you? Speak up, you redheaded numbskull.

That was then. I said *yes*. I said, *I do*. I said something in the affirmative.

My mother has turned ninety, and we are celebrating in Bonden. Her knees are giving her problems, but she is lucid and doesn't use a walker. Peg is there, and my mother introduces me to Irene. I have heard a lot about Irene on the telephone lately, and I pump her hand to show my enthusiasm. She is ninety-five. "Your mother and I," she tells me, "have had some really fun times together."

Mama Mia is writing poems at the kitchen table. The little Daisy girl is stirring in her crib.

Mia is in the hospital now, diagnosed with a brief psychosis, a transitory alienation of her reason, a brain glitch. She is officially *une folle*. She is writing in the notebook BRAIN SHARDS.

> 7.
> An insistent thing—
> but speechless,
> not identity,
> a waking dream that leaves no image,
> only agonies. I need a name.
> I need a word in this white world.
> I need to call it something, not nothing.
> Choose a picture from nowhere,
> from a hole in a mind
> and look, there on the ledge:
> A flowering bone.

11.
I blibe and bleeb on rovsty hobe
With Sentecrate, Bilt, and Frobe,
My buddles down from Iberbean,
The durkerst toon in Freen.

21.
Once over easy, love,
Twice over tough,
Piss and vinegar.
Turds and stout.
What's this all about?

She is sane again, and she is in the Burdas' living room reading a biography of that coy but passionate genius, the Danish philosopher who has been irking and unsettling and bewildering her for years. The date is August 19, 2009.

I have come round to myself, as you can see. Only a few days have passed since the funeral. I have come round to who I was then, during that summer I spent with my mother and the Swans and Lola and Flora and Simon and the young witches of Bonden. Abigail is lying in her grave on the outskirts of town. There is no stone yet. That will come later. It wasn't so long ago, after all, and my memory of that time is sharp. Daisy was still with me. In the days previous, the sixteenth, seventeenth, and eighteenth, Boris Izcovich had been wooing me in a steady, earnest manner and had even sent me an egregious but touching poem that began: "I knew a girl named Mia / who knew her rhyme and meter / And onomatopoeia." It fell off badly after that, but what can one expect from a world-renowned neuroscientist? The sentiment expressed after those introductory lines was, as described by Daisy, "total mush." That said, only the most hard-hearted among us have no use for mush or blarney or those old ballads about lost and dead lovers, and only bona fide dunces are unable to take pleasure in the stories of ghostly figures who wander across moors or fields or out in the open air. And who among us would deny Jane Austen her happy endings or insist that Cary Grant and Irene Dunne should not get back together at the end of *The Awful Truth*? There are tragedies and there are comedies, aren't there? And they are often more the same than different, rather like men and women, if you ask me. A comedy depends on stopping the story at exactly the right moment.

And I will tell you in all confidence, old friend, for that is what you are by now, Stalwart Reader, tested and true and so dear to me. I will tell you that the old man had been making inroads, as they say, and tromping closer and closer to whatever it was *in there*, in me, and the explanation was time, quite simply, time, all the time spent, and the daughter, who was born and loved and grew up into the kooky, kind, and gifted darling that she is, and all the talking and the fighting and the sex, too, between me and the big B., the memories of Sidney and my own Celia, who didn't need to be discovered by Columbus, I can vouch for that. And in my secret heart of hearts, I admit there was some old mush that hadn't been scooped out of me by hardship and insanity. But there was also the story itself, the story Boris and I had written together, and in that story, our bodies and thoughts and memories had gotten themselves so tangled up that it was hard to see where one person's ended and the other's began.

But back to the nineteenth of August 2009, late afternoon, around five o'clock. Flora was visiting with Moki, and Daisy was entertaining the two of them with a song-and-dance number. Flora was clapping wildly and encouraging Moki to do so as well. The weather was not good, a swamp of a day if ever there was one, ninety-five and bleary, mosquitoes on the loose after the rains. I was having some difficulty concentrating on my book, what with all the commotion, but I had finally come to Kierkegaard's broken engagement. He loved her. She loved him, and he BREAKS it off, only to suffer grotesque and exquisite mental tortures. What a sad and perverse adventure that was. When I noticed that Daisy had stopped singing, I looked up. She had turned toward the window.

"A car's coming up the driveway." She leaned toward the glass. "I can't see who it is. You're not expecting anybody, are you? Good Lord, he's getting out of the car. He's walking toward the steps. He's up the steps. He's ringing the bell." I heard the bell. "It's Dad, Mom. It's Dad! Well, well, aren't you going to answer it? What's the matter with you?"

Flora grabbed Daisy around the thighs and began to bounce up and down in anticipation. "Well?" she crowed. "Well?"

"You get it," I said. "Let him come to me."

FADE TO BLACK